I0596697

The Glass Ball

Jean Hatfield

Aleutika Press

© 2014 by Jean Hatfield
All rights reserved. Published by Aleutika Press. No part of this publication may be reproduced or distributed in any form or by any means, or stored in a database or retrieval system, without the prior written permission of the publisher.

Editing by Kristin Thiel, Susan DeFreitas, Laura Garwood Meehan, and Vinnie Kinsella
Cover image by Robert James Aston
Book design by Vinnie Kinsella
Printed in the United States of America

lookingforluke.com

ISBN: 978-0-9909223-0-8

To Ms. S. and to my husband,
with deepest love and gratitude

And to the courageous women who shared their stories
and the women who could have

Acknowledgments

This book would not have been possible without the assistance of Kristin Thiel, editor extraordinaire, who embraced my vision, artfully edited the manuscript, and guided me along the path to publication. I can't thank her enough.

Special thanks to Robyn Aston for his artistic genius—his beautiful cover photograph complements the story so well; to Vinnie Kinsella for his publishing expertise, creativity with the cover design and book layout, and editing; and to Susan DeFreitas and Laura Garwood Meehan for their superb editing skills. Thanks also to Laurie Rosin and Dale Gelfand for editing early versions. And I am very proud to thank my daughter, Mackenzie, for her inspired depiction of our beloved family dog, Allie, the Aleutika Press logo.

My heartfelt appreciation for the encouragement, support, and wisdom of my family and dear friends. From the many brainstorming sessions, sometimes at 4:00 a.m. and sometimes at midnight, to reading my manuscript and providing insightful feedback, and to sharing lots of ice cream, you have all been a vital part of this book's creation. There are too many of you to individually thank—you know who you are, and I love you all.

Prologue

It didn't take long after the death of Dana's dad for her mom to feel the strain of being the sole provider—financially and emotionally—for a young child. So when her husband's older brother offered to move in and help keep the household running, she didn't hesitate to say yes.

It must have been touching, really, in an old-fashioned way.

"Just don't try to marry me." As young as she was, Dana still caught her mother's comment, if not its joking delivery. The three of them were in the kitchen, already as normal a group to Dana as Dana, her mom, and her dad had once been. Her mom and uncle were drinking beer, and Dana was cross-legged on the linoleum, her mom absently braiding and undoing, braiding and undoing her hair. It felt so good. Dana was warm and sleepy and happy. Her uncle watched her, a light in his eyes.

"Mommy"—Dana managed a four-year-old's tone of exasperation—"you and Uncle can't get married! You're already…"

She struggled to say the cumbersome word *related*, but neither adult helped her, and the conversation carried on over her head.

More than twenty-five years later, that day would remain vivid for the little girl, now grown, and not even a memory for the man, now old. Alzheimer's spared him of his memories of what he did to her, while she had to find a way to free herself from hers.

Part One

Chapter One

SHE AWOKE WITH A START, STILL SMELLING THE SWEAT FROM HIS body as he loomed over her, still tasting the oil from the gun he had thrust into her mouth, still hearing the harsh ratcheting sound of the hammer being pulled back. Wild-eyed, heart pounding, her skin prickling with dread, she glanced frantically around the small, unfamiliar room. Was that movement she saw out of the corner of her eye? She felt the color drain from her face. Opening her mouth, she tried to call for help, but the words caught in her throat.

Then the framed print of Mount McKinley on the far wall came into focus, reminding Dana she was at a seaside inn in Alaska, far from her Oregon home, and she cried out with relief. Breathing deeply to dispel the enveloping, nearly paralyzing panic, she mouthed a silent prayer of thanks. He wasn't really there. She'd only been having a nightmare.

Only? How many times had she been afraid she wouldn't be able to climb out of the darkness when she awakened in its depths?

With great effort, Dana fought off the invisible pressure that seemed to weigh on her chest. She unfolded her tightly crossed arms and pulled herself upright. As she swung her feet off the bed, she realized her nightgown and hair were soaked with sweat. She shivered. Her nightmares were terrifying and real...and exhausting.

Willing herself to stand, Dana then donned the crumpled terry-cloth robe that a few hours earlier she had tossed onto the wicker chair next to the bed. Her journal was open on the nightstand, and the scribbled words, *I'm dying inside!*, screamed back at her. Quickly she closed the book, fresh tears spilling from her swollen eyes, and squeezed the paw of the small, well-worn stuffed animal she'd clung to while she slept.

Suddenly longing for fresh air, she walked toward the balcony of her second-story room. She opened the sliding door and stepped outside, grabbing the railing to steady herself. Moisture from the previous night's rain dampened the small wooden deck and tingled her bare feet. She gulped in the crisp, salty air, only vaguely aware of the seagull that called in passing and the cool breeze that played with the wisps escaping her long auburn braids. She stared, unseeing, across the wide bay that separated glaciers and mountains from the rocky beach beneath her, lost in another, earlier world—a world she was trying to forget.

"You can't let him win!" she chastised herself, speaking so softly she wasn't sure if she had actually spoken the words aloud. Feeling chilled, she pulled her robe tightly around her slender body—almost as if by doing so she could pull herself together as well. Wiping away another flood of tears, she closed her eyes, hoping to capture the serenity of the dawn. "Think of nothing. Breathe deeply. Relax." Dana whispered the words again and again like a mantra, struggling to shake off the images that flashed through her mind like stills from a movie. "Let those feelings go...you don't need them anymore." Unconsciously fingering the tight curl on the end of one of her braids, she concentrated on the words. The painful images slowly faded.

The muffled purr of a boat's engine roused Dana from her reverie. A sailboat, sails furled, was making its way under power out of the harbor, just off the steep beach in front of the inn. Lifting her gaze, she looked back across the bay at the towering snow-capped mountains, the jagged peaks tinged pink with sunrise and framed boldly against the slowly deepening blue sky. This time she focused on them as though they were talismans. Surely surrounded by such spectacular scenery she could find a few moments of cherished peace.

Exhaling deeply, she looked at her watch. She'd never get back to sleep now—not that she slept much anyway. She might as well begin her day. "A *new* day," she said with resolve.

As she started to walk back into her room, a deep voice yelled, "Be careful, boy!" Dana turned in time to see a large dog standing on the sailboat's bow, looking straight at her. The way this dog stared at her, with such intensity, reminded her of Lucky, her dog, who had died a few months before. And he reminded her just as much of Boots, her childhood dog. Dana had learned early in life to trust animals; unlike other bonds, that trust had never been compromised or destroyed. Her uncle had insisted Boots be an outside dog, but as often as she could, she had snuck Boots into the house late at night, sleeping with her arms wrapped around him, gathering strength from his warmth, love, and devotion. Those times when she awakened in the middle of the night, trembling with fear, he had licked her face, calming her. Never once had Boots let her down or hurt her. Now, this dog held her gaze until the sailboat disappeared from view.

On her way to the bathroom, Dana picked up her cell phone and called a number saved as *Moors* in her contacts.

"The Moors Residence and Hospice," a voice answered. Dana's response followed a script. She gave her uncle's name and her own and asked to be connected to his room. There was a short pause as the person found the extension, and then the voice replied, "Here you go."

As soon as the phone started ringing in her uncle's room, Dana hung up. She didn't regularly call the long-term care facility where her uncle had lived since her teenage years, when he developed early-onset Alzheimer's, but she did when she needed to. So young when his abuse had stopped, she hadn't thought until years later that she may not have been his only victim. By then he was under lock and key—though not the kind Dana wished for him—unable to hurt anyone else. Confirming that he was still there with a phone call to the front desk became a salve Dana applied whenever she was really anxious. She didn't need those feelings of panic and fear anymore because he could not get her—he could not get anyone.

Dana headed to the bathroom, where she threw off her robe and peeled her damp nightgown off her shivering body. After unbraiding her hair, she adjusted the water as hot as she could stand it and stepped into the shower. Would she ever warm up? She supposed she could have chosen differently with her travel plans. But Alice, the inn's proprietor, had assured Dana it was the perfect place to thaw.

"In fact," she said as Dana greeted her later that morning, "I've signed you up for some time in the sun—a kayak trip leaving from the lobby in about an hour."

"You what?" Dana laughed. Under any circumstances, she would have had a difficult time being angry at Alice, a woman with soft eyes and a quick smile who looked about the age Dana's mother would have been, had she not died a couple of years before from a heart attack. But Alice and Dana also shared a profession, and Dana had performed the same sort of "activity matchmaking" for the guests of the bed-and-breakfast she co-owned with her friend Andrea. It was one of the reasons Dana had gotten into the hospitality business: she loved helping people escape into their dreams, but many times people were too close to see what those dreams were and needed a wise outsider's nudge.

And thank goodness for nudges. If her therapist hadn't applauded Dana's idea to take a sabbatical north, Dana may never have fulfilled her dream, though it was a dream born of a nightmare. Growing up in Seattle, she was well aware of Alaska, watching the many ships—passenger and freight—leave her port city for the state magnified in her imagination. She never knew which boats were headed north, but she liked to think they all were. Her grandparents had taken a ferry to Alaska once, so she had known it was possible. Her seven-year-old mind had had it all figured out, even the part where she smuggled herself on board. On a ferry it would be easy to blend in with the passengers, she had reasoned at the time. She had taken enough local ferries to know she could simply hang out on the upper decks, pretending to be some adult passenger's child. Maybe she could even come aboard with a family with a bunch of kids—people probably wouldn't notice one more.

Looking through *National Geographic* magazine photos, pinning maps to her bedroom wall, and tracing her finger along Alaska's craggy coastline, she had idealized its pristine beauty, quiet expanse, and seemingly endless distance from her home. All of these things made it the sanctuary of her dreams. There was no way her uncle could find her in Alaska. No one could. And just once, if only for a little while, she wanted to go somewhere so remote that no one could find her—an actual place, and not one of the faraway havens of her imagination.

Every June when she was young she'd had an all too brief escape to her grandparents' house on the Oregon coast, though she dreaded the arrival of August when her mother came to take her home. She always asked her grandparents if she could just stay, assuring them she wouldn't mind leaving all her friends at school and that she was sure she'd make new friends in Oregon, but Grandma just smiled and slid another grilled cheese sandwich onto her plate, and Grandpa just smiled and ruffled her hair and said what a lucky girl she was to be growing up with a mom who loved her in a city as magical as Seattle.

Mark's family lived next door, and Dana spent almost as much time there as she did at her grandparents' house. Mark was a couple of years older than she was, and they'd liked each other from the start. For Dana, the bonus that came along with being Mark's best summer friend was that she got to hang out as a part of his big family. Coming from her house, where she was an only child and felt she had nowhere to hide, being one of six rambunctious kids (all boys, except for her) felt so good. Even before Dana confessed to Mark how scared she was at home, he knew she didn't like how alone she was in Seattle. He was the one who suggested she make her own family of stuffed animals, surrounding herself with them in bed, at the dinner table, wherever and whenever she wanted. She could even hide a couple in her school backpack. That was how Brownie, the well-loved teddy bear she'd brought with her to Alaska, had come to be such a good friend. Dana still took comfort in what he symbolized.

Mark as a boy had been full of good ideas, like when he suggested the stuffed-animal family. Now as an adult and Dana's boyfriend, he encouraged Dana to seek therapy, all the while remaining supportive.

"You need more help than I can give you," he told her once after she confessed in a quiet voice to experiencing suicidal thoughts, "but I will never leave you." When she had panic attacks, when she retreated into her room with depression, when she couldn't stand his touch—let alone sex—he stayed by her side. "We're about more than sex," he said. "We're best friends and partners. And I would never want you to do anything that makes you feel uncomfortable. You went through hell, but you're not there anymore. You're here, with me."

Mark had been the one to remind Dana about Alaska. Dana had been making slow but steady progress with her therapist and Mark's tenderness, but after the emotional stress of her mom's sudden death, Dana's nightmares started recurring more regularly and more vividly than ever before. She'd had setbacks before—just when she'd start to think her trauma was finally behind her, it would burst into her life again without warning, an erupting volcano of sensations, feelings, and memories. This last time, though, it had virtually overtaken her, like molten lava. Lucky had done her best, just as Boots had before her, but they could only do so much. Everyone could only do so much. Watching her become increasingly unable to focus on anything else, Mark suggested a change of scenery. Dana warmed to the idea when both her therapist and Andrea (even though it was summer and the busiest time of year for their B and B) agreed wholeheartedly.

"I don't know about leaving you for so long," Dana had confessed as she and Mark embraced in the Portland airport.

"You won't be. You'll send me emails," he said, smiling, "and I...well, check the front pocket of your backpack."

"What did you...?" Dana kept her smile on him as she fumbled in her bag. Her fingers soon pulled free a small envelope.

"I may have hidden a few more around your luggage. I want you to take control of the communication—I don't want to accidentally end up bugging you while you're trying to focus, so I'm not going to email you...okay, I'm going to try to refrain from emailing you! Unless you message me first. But I also don't want to just abandon you. There are notes from me, if and when you want them."

Dana threw her arms around Mark and kissed him good-bye. "And that's just one of the reasons why I love you," she said.

Eight hours later, after flying to Anchorage and connecting with a small commuter airline, Dana stepped off the plane at her destination, a small coastal town in Southcentral Alaska. She found her checked luggage and accepted the first taxi she saw. She was thankful to have found a room at an inn by the water's edge near the small boat harbor. The long summer days complemented her sleeping patterns: little sleep, lots of wakeful hours. And in those first few days she found herself spending most of her waking hours walking the beach, hoping to recreate the feeling of tranquility she had found at her grandparents' house. But instead of finding peace, instead of even beginning to figure out how to let her memories go, it seemed as if she had only run away.

She wrote emails to Mark about that—sometimes long and plaintive, sometimes short and exhausted—and he wrote back that he loved her and to give it time. She opened the first note of his, the one he'd directed her to in the airport: *I hope you find what you're looking for. I'll wait. For as long as it takes.* Whatever *it takes.* Yet the tenacious images pursued her, increasingly preying on her mind and spirit, haunting her—most viciously at night.

"I can tell you haven't been sleeping," Alice was saying to Dana now, after the latest restless night, which only ended with her call to her uncle's room, "and Jeff's kayak trip will cure that. Fresh air, a little bit of exercise, a lot of sunshine, the lull of the water beneath you, and it's even going to be a very low tide today, if you guys want to dig some clams...go!"

Dana felt her feet obeying Alice's shooing motion, and soon she was meeting Jeff and the other sightseers, and then she was floating.

And then she was happy.

She was…happy. Dana felt as if she had finally attained, if only temporarily, the respite she had desperately prayed for. The breathtaking scenery and its grandeur chased away her torment and conflicting emotions. She felt like a new person—or a person renewed.

"Hey, Jeff!" Dana called. She framed another scenic shot in her camera's viewfinder. "Can you wait up a minute?" She clicked the shutter and smiled at the results. No touchup or filter necessary.

Her group was floating along a winding shoreline, their brightly colored kayaks vivid against the water and dwarfed by the mountains. Carved by retreating glaciers, the fjord they were exploring was the largest in a series of inlets, coves, and bays that defined the coastline across from the town where Dana had sought refuge.

Jeff grinned. "Again?" He motioned to the others. "Okay, gang, let's drift. Besides, it doesn't get any better than this," he declared, gesturing toward the sweeping vista. From the tree line to the water's edge, the craggy mountains surrounding the bay were densely covered with old-growth spruce and alder. Framed by a startlingly blue sky, the peaks wore patches of stubborn snow, despite it being July. The shoreline was steep and rocky, occasionally widening to a narrow beach or small cove, and gentle waves lapped lazily against the shore.

Dana rejoined the others just as a woman named Amy was pointing excitedly. Two sleek, brown, furry creatures were floating on the water's surface about a hundred feet ahead of them. "Look!" Amy exclaimed. "Are those otters?"

"Sure are," Jeff confirmed.

The playful sea otters rolled and somersaulted in the water, heedless of the intruders in their midst. Their thick fur shimmered in the sunlight. As the kayakers paddled closer, Dana could see one had a baby riding on its belly.

Dana raised her Nikon and started clicking away. She could feel their carefree attitude fluttering her way. She was so absorbed with taking photographs that it took her a moment to realize Jeff had been talking to her.

"Tell you what, Dana," he said, "just past this island there's a wide beach, on the right. We'll stop for lunch, and you can meet up with us there."

"Great!" Dana said, not taking her eye from the Nikon's viewfinder. "Thanks, Jeff." She certainly was glad she'd taken Alice's advice. Jeff was right—the day couldn't get any better than this.

"Just don't get too near the island, though," Jeff cautioned. "Sitka might eat you alive."

Concentrating on her shot, Dana waved absently, barely aware of Jeff's words.

The otters disappeared twenty photographs later. Dana snapped the lens cap on her camera and rested her paddle across the top of the kayak, drinking in the scene. Although this was kids' stuff compared to the river kayaking Mark was used to, he would appreciate the commanding beauty of the area. Her heart filled with love for him as she drifted the length of the small island, surveying its terrain with interest and thinking how much he would have enjoyed kayaking there. She wished he could be there with her. She knew he would have swapped his work schedule had she asked him, but they both knew she needed to do this alone.

The island appeared relatively flat and heavily wooded. A carpet of moss-covered soil overhung the rocky perimeter. Heavy roots, extending from the majestic spruce trees clinging to the shallow soil near the edge of the island, jutted out into space from under the overhanging soil carpet. As Dana examined the shoreline, she noticed the island had the appearance of a single great rock rising out of the water, ringed by rocky beaches that she could see through the clear water beneath her kayak. Though much of the shore was too steep to climb easily, in several places the kelp-and-barnacle-covered rock face sloped down more gently to the beach below. Here and there, natural terraces in the sloping rock had formed; some contained small tide pools full of sea life, created by the dramatic tidal range in the area.

As Dana wondered who or what this "Sitka" was that Jeff had warned her about, she stowed her Nikon, wanting to experience the beauty around her through her own eyes rather than through the lens of her camera. Her senses were heightened as a flood of impressions flowed over her: the unparalleled beauty, the solitude, the tranquility, the quiet…

She sighed with deep contentment and paddled past a small cove littered with clamshells. As she rounded the end of the island, relaxing in the warm and soothing sunshine, she pictured herself as a little girl walking along the beach below her grandparents' house, listening to the waves break on the shore, inhaling the salty ocean fragrance, and squishing the soft sand between her toes while scouring the tide line for shells. She remembered how happy and safe she had felt—for those few brief weeks, anyway. Now she suddenly felt she had found what she had been searching for—another haven where her torment disappeared—and miraculously she was at peace with herself.

She closed her eyes and drifted in her floating cocoon. She was so completely unburdened, she wished she could suspend time and live in this moment forever.

As the kayak bumped to a gentle stop against the edge of one of the seaweed-covered rock terraces exposed by the low tide, a deep *woof* interrupted Dana's meditation. She opened her eyes, blinking to make sure she wasn't imagining the stunning creature lying on the rocks before her, his eyes level with hers. He was the most magnificent dog she had ever seen—and surely the largest. His slate-gray fur was so bushy and full, he looked like an oddly colored bear cub.

Two piercing yellow eyes stared directly at her. She gasped. "You're the dog I saw on the sailboat this morning!" The dog cocked his head and then rested it on his paws. Smiling, Dana reached out to pet him.

"Ahhh, *you* must be Sitka," she said, rubbing his ears. Dana was captivated. She loved dogs, almost more than people, her mom used to say. "You don't look so ferocious to me," she declared.

Contentedly petting the beautiful dog, Dana fell quiet and could hear the barnacles crackling as the receding tide left them exposed. She looked around. The trees were less dense on this end of the island, and she noticed a house rising dramatically above the steep rocks. Her eyes widened. "Sitka, do you live here? How lucky you are!"

Sitka placed his paw on Dana's arm and licked her face. She smiled and wrapped her arms around his neck, then scratched behind his ears. She buried her face in his thick fur. "You're a sweetheart," she murmured.

She snuggled with the dog for a few more seconds and then sighed and sat up. "I've got to go now, Sitka. But first let me take your picture." She was imagining his photo in a frame by her bed. A fitting memento of a memorable day—and yet another marvelous dog in her life, even if only for a moment. After taking two shots, she hugged Sitka good-bye, pushed away from the rocks, and began paddling.

She glanced over her shoulder as she neared the beach where the other kayakers waited. Sitka was still lying in the same place, watching her.

Chapter Two

It was evening by the time the group arrived back at the harbor. Begging off the invitation to join the other kayakers for dinner, Dana said her good-byes and left the group at Jeff's boat slip. Walking up the ramp, she shook her head in bemusement as she remembered the bet Amy and Mandy had made as to which one could finagle a date with Jeff. Laughing, they'd invited her to join them in the wager, and she'd passed, though she hadn't explained why. The main reason, of course, was Mark. But even if she hadn't had a boyfriend or been trying to concentrate on her inner peace, she probably wouldn't have gone along with the antics. Because of her wariness of men other than Mark, Dana had shied away from the dating scene. She truly felt very lucky to have had Mark for all these years, first as a best friend and then as her boyfriend.

That night she sent Mark four photos from the excursion—a couple of the scenery, one of Sitka, and one of herself. She wrote only *I love you*. She knew the email was the equivalent of a "wish you were here" postcard, but for the first time since arriving in Alaska, she didn't feel like explaining more. She felt a new and creeping joy that she needed to process on her own. She hoped Mark would be able to read her mood in the photos, especially in the way the afternoon sunlight in the one of her made her skin glow. *I'm alive,* she hoped the photo told him. She didn't quite understand why she herself couldn't tell him that.

Dana lay down in bed, but sleep wouldn't come. This time, though, it was not because anxiety plagued her but because it was still light out and she felt energized. The solitude and beauty of her kayaking trip had renewed Dana's energy and her spirit. From now on *she* was going to be in control, not her past. She felt a new resolve to fit the fragmented pieces of her life into a well-meshed whole. She needed to, for herself—and for Mark and their future, if they were going to have one.

She got up and used the bathroom. She smiled as she washed her hands, once again appreciating the sign stuck on the mirror over the sink: *NO FISH IN THE BATHTUB!!* As she made her way quietly down the stairs to take advantage of the beautiful evening for a walk, she wondered about the smelly event that had prompted posting that sign.

She wandered back toward the harbor, where the fishing fleet stood silent and unmanned, the crews of the charter boats home for a few hours of well-deserved rest before repeating their daily routine. Each morning she watched the procession of boats motor past her window, the long line traveling together to the popular fishing grounds. She generally met them when they returned in late afternoon, sometimes taking pictures of the fishermen with their prized catches. The biggest halibut she'd seen so far weighed over three hundred pounds, though a young boy she met on one of her forays told her the smaller ones tasted better.

Dana walked aimlessly up and down the docks. The tranquility that had replaced the daytime hubbub calmed her and at the same time stimulated her senses. The faint smell of fish lingered at the cleaning stations. A dog yipped in the distance. Raucous laughter spilled briefly from the tavern near the general store when someone opened the door. The air was crisp and cool. Dana shoved her hands into the pockets of her windbreaker and turned back toward the inn.

Walking along the beach, she neared the bar attached to the inn's restaurant and was drawn by the sound of music coming from inside. There was often a band playing in the evening, but tonight's was especially compelling. When her mom remarried and her uncle left, Dana had started taking piano lessons, a "thank you for welcoming me to your family" gift from her new stepfather. At first she'd been on edge, unhappy about having to accept any gift from any man, but she had to admit that her stepfather didn't look at her the way her uncle did, and he certainly never touched her the way her uncle did or threatened her. The intriguing piano melody coming from the Mariner, identified by the beautifully carved driftwood sign above the door, was accompanied by bluesy guitar accents.

Just as she reached the deck outside the Mariner, something heavy collided with her legs. The dog from the island!

"I'm happy to see you too, Sitka!" Dana laughed and obligingly scratched his stomach when he flopped down and rolled onto his back. Petting Sitka further relaxed Dana; she had connected with this gorgeous creature from the moment he had first looked into her eyes.

Now she knelt and talked to Sitka as if he were a trusted friend she could confide in. "So, were you just sitting here listening to the music? It must be good, then. Mind if I join you?"

Sitka whined happily.

"Thanks, new pal." Dana sat down next to the dog, who had resettled on the deck. "I'm not much for bars, so this is the best seat in the house, in my opinion."

Dana closed her eyes, refocusing her mind as she stroked Sitka's fur and listened to the music. She needed to sit down at a piano again. She needed to call her stepfather again. He reminded her of Mark, and just as Mark had become de facto family to her, so had her stepfather. He was so gentle and concerned. She'd never told him what her uncle had done to her—only Mark and her therapist knew any of that—but he seemed to sense a deep wound. He had never pushed her into any particular hobby or career path but had always encouraged her in everything in which she'd expressed interest. In the same way as Mark was purposefully not initiating communication with her now, her stepfather had tried not to intrude on her life, especially once her mother died. Since then, they'd exchanged only a handful of phone calls, at birthdays and holidays, and no visits. But just because he was ignorant of her pain—his ignorance being her own doing, she knew—and had entered her life during a time she would rather forget did not mean they could not be good friends, could not be the lifelong family her mother had wanted them to be.

"You're the only other person Sitka's ever let hug him like that."

Startled, Dana looked up and saw a tall man standing before her with an amused look on his face and a guitar in his hand.

"He's a beautiful dog," Dana murmured, her body partially hidden by Sitka's own. "I've never seen one like him."

The man's voice was gentle. "You must be pretty special."

Dana quickly stood up, declining his offer of assistance with a shake of her head. She brushed off her jeans with one hand while Sitka nuzzled the other. "Well, maybe not that special. Sitka and I actually met before—earlier today, while I was out kayaking."

"Oh! A Jeff group? You passed right by my island then. Sitka let you close, on his home turf? Definitely pretty special." He extended his arm again. "Luke MacFarland."

This time Dana clasped his hand. His touch was warm and unexpectedly comforting. "I'm Dana Montgomery."

"Pleased to meet you." Luke smiled and held her gaze with kind eyes the color of a robin's egg.

"Nice to meet you too," Dana replied. "I've been enjoying the music." Suddenly disconcerted by the compelling yet calming aura emanating from this stranger, Dana lowered her eyes and withdrew her hand. She fought the strong impulse to flee and decided instead to take her time leaving so as not to appear rude.

"You live in the most peaceful spot on earth."

Luke grinned.

"I'm new here," she tried to explain. "And just visiting."

"You're right about where I live." He smiled away her fumbling. He removed his baseball cap and ran his fingers through his thick sandy-colored hair. "How has your visit been so far?"

She smiled, relaxing a little, though her mind asked the fleeting question: why hadn't she just said good-bye and walked away? Luke was a very handsome man, but unlike Jeff, he didn't read like a playboy. He read like someone she could relax with. And that wasn't her plan. Because of Mark and because of herself. She waved a hand at the bay. "I've never seen such spectacular scenery. Just what the doctor ordered, as they say."

"You know what else the doctor orders? Food. I have to play the encore—I just came out to check on Sitka—but after that would you like to join me for a bite to eat?"

"Thank you, but no."

"Beer?" he persisted.

She shook her head. "I don't drink. Not much anyway."

Sitka licked Dana's hand, tickling her fingers.

"Look at him." Luke gestured at Sitka. "He won't leave you alone. I've never seen him like this. You've really won him over. No small feat, let me tell you. He's normally standoffish toward people, and his size can be intimidating."

"He does look like a small gray bear," Dana said. *Like a distant relative of Brownie.* The connection her mind made startled her. She reluctantly disengaged herself from Sitka. All of a sudden, she wanted to be alone, even as she found herself thinking that Luke was quite a disarming man. "Listen, I've really got to go."

Luke touched her arm lightly, not seeming to notice when she pulled away. "Are you here for a while?"

"A little while." Dana nodded as Sitka stretched, sat up, and demanded attention by placing his paw on her arm.

"Well, it was nice meeting you." From inside came the sound of Luke's bandmates tuning their instruments. "Guess that's my cue," he said and turned to go back inside. "I won't be long. I hope you decide to hang around with Sitka."

Chapter Three

THE ENCORE ENDED, AND LUKE QUICKLY PACKED UP HIS GUITAR, anxious to get outside and see if Dana was still there. Hopping off the stage, he gave a wave to the tavern keeper. "See ya, Jake," he called.

As he made his way through the bar, he mentally shook his head. What had gotten into him? Usually he kept to himself around women; yet after their chance meeting, he would have talked with Dana for hours—hell, all night—and hoped she gave him the chance. Yet suddenly he felt a pang in his heart and was uncertain whether he really wanted her to be waiting for him.

He reached the door and pushed it open. Sitka was alone. "She really did call it a night, huh, boy?"

Sitka wagged his tail in response.

Luke stepped over to the deck railing and looked up and down the beach, but it was deserted. The intensity of his disappointment surprised him. Why was he so attracted to her? He hadn't been interested in another woman since Jamie died, hadn't even given anyone a second glance. What was it about Dana that touched him so deeply?

He rummaged in his guitar case for his tablature pad, ripped out a piece, and wrote a short note, the words looking like exotic notes on the six-line staves.

"Come on, Sitka, let's see if we can find our new friend." He thought Dana had given an almost imperceptible nod toward the attached inn when she said she had to be going. "We need to find Alice." Even if Dana wasn't staying there, Alice knew where every resident lived and every visitor stayed.

He greeted the young man staffing the front desk and headed back into Alice's cluttered office. He found her sitting at her desk, surrounded by mounds of paperwork.

"Well, hello, stranger!" Alice's weathered face crinkled into a huge grin as she looked at Luke affectionately. "What can I do for you, dear?"

Luke wrapped Alice in a bear hug. "What do you know about Dana Montgomery?"

"She has good taste—she's staying here."

Luke grinned. Bingo! "And?" he prompted.

"Well...not much. She's been here just over a week." The innkeeper was thoughtful as she looked directly into Luke's eyes. "I think something is troubling her."

"What makes you say that?"

"She's always alone, and she walks the beach constantly, at all hours of the day and night. Taking pictures, usually. I suspect she hides behind that camera. I mean, how many sunset photographs do you need?"

"I *like* sunset photographs," he declared and held out his note to Alice. "Could you please give her this?" He then added sheepishly, "Uh, and do you have an envelope?"

Alice slowly reached for the paper and nodded. "I'll see that she gets it. And don't worry; I won't peek."

Dana lay in bed feeling terribly confused. If she hadn't bolted, she'd be having dinner with Luke right now, and she had to admit she half wished she were. What was it about this man that caused her to lower her defenses? She didn't understand what she was feeling or why. She certainly never expected to respond to a man the way she had to Luke. Ever since her nightmares had returned with regularity, she had even shied away from *Mark*. It was obvious she needed to avoid Luke for the rest of her visit. But that shouldn't be too hard, she reasoned; he lived on a remote island, after all.

She closed her eyes and fell into the most restful sleep she'd had in a long time. When she woke the next morning, she didn't believe the bedside clock and had to check her cell phone to confirm. Eight o'clock? Dana jumped out of bed, her heart thumping, and then she laughed out loud. Eight o'clock! She had slept a full night's sleep! She pulled on clothes, grabbed her camera, and stepped to her door.

She noticed an envelope on the floor just inside the door. Brow furrowed, Dana stooped and picked it up. It was addressed to her, simply, by her first name. She didn't recognize the handwriting. Inside was a sheet of music composition paper.

Dana,
How about dinner tomorrow night? 7:00? Boat slip a-15
Luke

Dana continued her path downstairs, but now in a bit of a flustered fog.

"Dana! Good morning," came a familiar voice.

"Alice," Dana said, focusing on the woman behind the front desk. She cleared her throat. "Did someone drop off—"

"Good, you saw the note. I slipped it under your door last night after Luke gave it to me. I know you're usually awake then, but I didn't want to knock, just in case you were sleeping." Alice's eyes widened. "I hope I didn't wake you!"

"No, I didn't see it till this morning," Dana said.

"Good." Alice smiled. "You know, Dana, you can trust Luke," she said, startling Dana, making Dana feel as though her thoughts from last night—and, though she was embarrassed to admit it even to herself, from this morning again—had been read. "He's one of the many strays I've adopted over the years. He stands out from the rest, however. He's honest, generous to a fault, and extremely loyal. He won't hurt you. Maybe he can help you find what you're searching for. And maybe you can help *him*."

Chapter Four

Dana saw Luke and Sitka before they saw her. She willed the butterflies in her stomach to go away and told herself she wouldn't stay long. She'd have dinner. That was all. Just like having dinner with friends at home. She remembered Luke's beautiful guitar playing. Okay, maybe she'd ask Luke to play a couple of songs. But then she'd leave. Simple as that.

Sitka must have heard Dana's approach, for he yipped and ran to meet her, almost knocking her down. She laughed and gave him a hug. "It's good to see you too, Sitka."

She looked over at Luke, who was smiling broadly. He approached the rail and offered his hand. "Hi, Dana!" His reassuring grip steadied her as he helped her onto the deck. "Welcome aboard the *Warm Breeze*."

"She's beautiful!" Dana exclaimed as she stepped onto the deck. "And I love the name. I could use a warm breeze. I haven't been able to warm up since I got here."

"I was thinking of calling her the *Cool Breeze*, but my wife never liked that. Jamie said people always think of Alaska as just a block of ice, and we needed to remind people that summer does arrive, short though it may be. Now I really like the name. I've felt nothing but warmth from this beauty."

"Your wife?" Dana asked. She hoped her question sounded casual. Why shouldn't he have a wife? And why would it concern her? She had an absolutely wonderful boyfriend who adored her, though she often wished he didn't treat her quite so much as if she were a fragile doll.

Luke's smile was small. "No wife, no girlfriend. I was married. She died three years ago."

"Oh! Oh, Luke, I'm so sorry."

He opened his mouth as though to say something but closed it quickly, this time into a brighter smile. "I loved her—I will always love her. I'm lucky I got to spend what time I did with her, and I've found peace again. There are days, moments, though..." Luke looked away. "But I'm finally ready to move on."

Dana felt herself nod, and not just to indicate she was listening—she was really hearing him. Moving on from the past...

Luke cleared his throat and said lightly, "Have you done any sailing?"

"Just a little," Dana said. "Years ago." Another interest of hers that her stepfather had supported. "How big is the *Warm Breeze*?"

"Thirty-two feet. Would you like something to drink?"

They had reached the salon, and Dana sat down at the table, feeling, to her relief, relaxed. *So far, so good.*

"A 7UP, if you have it."

Luke pulled a can of Sprite from the small fridge. Dana smiled and nodded her approval, and he poured it into a coffee mug. "Ceramic's a little sturdier than glass when choppy waters catch you off guard," he explained as he handed her the mug. "As for dinner, I hope you haven't had your fill of halibut yet."

"I don't think I could. It's so delicious." Dana sipped her soft drink and studied the cabin interior. "The woodwork is beautiful," she said, running her hand along the teak trim.

"Thanks." Luke removed two filets from the fridge.

"Was the boat built up here?" Dana asked.

"No. By a wooden-boat builder in the San Juan Islands. Sailed her up from there. I got Sitka on that trip. Found him wandering around some hot springs close to the town of Sitka." Luke pulled a box of matches from a drawer and walked to the dinette. "He's pretty much my family now."

"And wonderful family he is," she said aloud, ruffling the fur on Sitka's head.

Luke lit the polished-brass kerosene lantern that hung from a beam above the gimbaled table. A warm glow spread throughout the cabin. "Well, I do also have my mom, who's in San Diego, but I can't stand my stepfather, so I don't see her as much as I would like. I've never liked the way he treats her. He's always been a mean drunk." Luke selected a knife and continued to speak thoughtfully as he cut the fish with precise care. "Anyway, I left Southern California to get away from him and hitchhiked north, working along the way, and finally wound up here."

"And your father?" Dana asked, not sure what else to say.

"He died about ten years ago. He and I weren't close either. I wanted us to be, even hitchhiked to Chicago the summer I turned fourteen to see him. I thought my dad would be overjoyed to see me, and everything would be okay, and I wouldn't have to go back and live with my stepfather. Well, my dad was happy to see me, but I couldn't stay with him. His business took up all of his time, and his girlfriend couldn't be bothered with me." For the second time that evening, Luke cleared his throat. "Listen, I'm going to poach the fish in dry white wine and tarragon. How about some rice too?"

"Sounds great," Dana said quickly and quietly. This was not the dinnertime conversation she had anticipated having. Was he this frank with everyone? Or maybe it was because she was a total stranger—who would soon drift out of his life as quickly as she had drifted into it—that made it easy for him to reveal himself.

As if reading her thoughts, Luke said, "I'm sorry if I made you feel uncomfortable. I didn't mean to—"

"No, not at all," Dana assured him, at the same time admitting to herself she wasn't sure *how* she felt. About what he said. About *him*. She stood up and looked around the cabin. "Don't wooden boats take a lot of extra care?"

Luke nodded. "Yeah, they do. But wooden boats are alive and have their own personality. In fact, if you listen, a wooden boat talks to you. With each point of sail, and as the force of the wind and waves change, it moans and creaks differently. The pull of the helm and the way the heel changes are unique. I think of the *Warm Breeze* as part of my family too." He finished cutting the halibut and set a pan of water on the stove to boil.

"What can I do to help?" Dana asked.

"You could set the table. The silverware is in the third drawer down. And toss the salad. The tomatoes are from Jake's greenhouse—a real treat, let me tell you. Jake runs the bar where I played last night."

As she carried out the simple tasks, Dana knew she should marvel over tomatoes grown in Alaska, but instead she wondered about the circumstances of Luke's wife's death three years earlier. She also wondered why he didn't have a girlfriend. He was friendly, charming, and talented. And a great lead in the kitchen. For the next thirty minutes, they worked effortlessly together, Luke as the chef and Dana assisting.

The plates filled and Dana seated, Luke presented a bottle of Rochioli sauvignon blanc, a dish towel draped over his arm. "Some wine, mademoiselle?"

Hesitating for the barest moment, Dana laughed. "Just a sip," she said.

"Been saving this for a special occasion." Luke found a

corkscrew and pulled out the cork. He then poured the wine into two fluted wineglasses. "I borrowed these glasses from Jake. Pretty fancy, huh? I don't do much entertaining, other than having a few beers with Jake now and then." Luke handed Dana her glass and held out his for a toast. "To Sitka, for introducing us."

Dana smiled and tapped her glass against Luke's. "To Sitka." At the sound of his name, Sitka approached the table and leaned against Dana while she petted his head and flank. With her other hand, she picked up her fork and flaked off a bite of fish. "Delicious!" she pronounced.

"Glad you think so. By the way, if you ever go halibut fishing, leave your bananas at home."

Dana's eyes narrowed. "My *bananas*?" she asked, unable to suppress a laugh.

"Don't laugh at me, lady," Luke chided. "This is serious stuff here. A friend of mine is a charter boat captain, and one day he was fishing in an area where all the other boats were catching halibut right and left. Not a single person on his boat even had a bite. Desperate, he finally asked if anyone had brought a banana in their lunch. Turns out a woman from Albuquerque had. 'Throw it overboard! *Now!*' my friend told her. 'They're bad luck!'"

Dana giggled.

"You're mocking me," Luke chastised her good-naturedly. "But as soon as the woman threw her banana overboard, they started catching one fish after another and limited out in no time. Caught the biggest halibut of the day too: a hundred and eighty pounder."

"Okay, I'm convinced," Dana said, throwing up her hands in concession. "No bananas!"

"You'll love this story too," Luke said. "I saved the best for last." He refilled his wineglass before continuing. Dana had hardly touched hers.

"Jake was fishing with a couple of friends, not too far from my place. He was reeling in what he thought was a whopper of a halibut when an orca surfaced with the fish in its mouth."

"You're kidding!"

"Nope. He's got some great pictures. Anyway, the whale chomped the fish, spit it out, and then swam right next to the boat. Jake said the orca was so close he could have stepped onto its back."

"Wow, that's an incredible story!" Dana said. "I'd love to see an orca."

"I might be able to arrange something," Luke said, looking intently at her.

Discomfited by the hopeful look evident in Luke's penetrating blue eyes, Dana stared at the floor. Why didn't she just tell him about Mark, thank him for the nice evening, and leave? Instead she asked, "Are these dark strips in the floor made of teak?"

"Yep. And the light strips are holly." Luke cleared the table and put the dishes in the sink to soak.

"Holly? As in holly berries?"

Luke nodded.

"It's beautiful. I never knew holly could be used as a building material."

Luke knelt next to Sitka and buried his hands in his fur. "Jamie and I designed the *Warm Breeze* ourselves."

"How long did it take to build?"

"Seemed like forever—a full year from start to finish. Jamie died soon after the boat was completed. I almost sold the *Warm Breeze* at that point. It didn't feel right to sail her without Jamie." Luke's voice filled with sadness, and Dana followed his gaze to a carving of a bald eagle on the forward bulkhead. "But I couldn't bring myself to sell her, either. After about a year, I finally decided to sail to Alaska."

Dana stood and walked over to the eagle Luke had been looking at. "This is magnificent," she said, running her fingers over the body. "I've never seen anything like it. What's it made of?"

"A lot of things. The body is solid teak, but its head is ash, and the claws and beak are pine. The tail feathers are birch. It was a wedding gift from Jake." Luke paused and then added, "A nesting pair of bald eagles returns every year to the island. Seems like you can always spot an eagle perched high in the trees across the narrow channel from the house, as if they're keeping you company. And you frequently hear their call, even when you can't see them." He met Dana's gaze, and they both smiled. "Would you like to take a walk on the beach?"

Dana glanced at her watch and was startled to see how late it was. The time had flown by. Her resolve to leave early was gone. "Yes, I'd love to." The eagerness with which Dana replied surprised her.

Luke followed her up the companionway through the hatch and onto the deck. Sitka bounded up the ladder behind them. Luke then helped Dana step onto the dock, and the threesome made their way to the beach.

The short Alaskan summer night was settling on the bay, shading everything in muted blues and purples. The light breeze smelled of salt and kelp, and a lone seagull skimmed the water as it headed to shore.

Dana's and Luke's rubber boots crunched on the beach gravel as they followed Sitka. He was bounding ahead of them, running up and down along the water's edge, digging holes in the soft, wet sand exposed by the outgoing tide.

"My dog used to do that," Dana said, enjoying watching Sitka as he enjoyed himself. "She was a stray who adopted me." Dana bent over and picked up a long strand of red seaweed. "Lucky for me. That's what I named her: Lucky. I took her everywhere. Every morning we walked on the beach below my house." Dana's mind turned also to Boots—already Sitka felt to her as much of a protector and friend as both of her dogs had been.

"You don't have Lucky anymore?" Luke asked as they sat down on a large piece of driftwood.

Dana shook her head. "She died a few months ago."

"I'm sorry," Luke said quietly.

"I miss her a lot."

Sitka finally tired. He ambled over and flopped down in front of Dana, nuzzling her hand. Dana touched her cheek to the top of his head and scratched his left ear. He groaned with pleasure.

"You sure do have a way with animals," Luke said in admiration.

"Well, I love dogs," Dana replied and then kissed Sitka on his long snout. "And they love you no matter what."

"Man's—and woman's—best friend," Luke replied in agreement.

They fell into comfortable silence. The faint smell of smoke from a bonfire wafted down the beach. Muted voices could be heard coming from backpackers' tents clustered near the fire. A bald eagle called in the distance, and the breaking waves lapped the shore.

Dana broke the silence. "Would you play your guitar for me?"

"Sure thing." Luke helped Dana to her feet.

They returned to the *Warm Breeze*, and Luke went below for his guitar while Dana sat on deck and savored the quiet. The still air enveloped her like a soft blanket. Sitka settled at her feet and immediately fell into a deep sleep, his legs occasionally twitching as he dreamed.

"Sitka probably thinks he's still running on the beach," Dana said as Luke emerged through the hatch with his guitar.

"Yeah, apparently it's his favorite activity whether he's awake or not." He held up the instrument. "Any special requests?"

"Something soothing and relaxing would be nice."

"Let me see…" Luke plucked the guitar strings. "Here's a song I wrote that might be just the ticket. Haven't played it in a long time."

Dana removed her boots and stretched out on the cushioned cockpit seat, gazing up at the darkening sky with her hand resting on Sitka's head. As she breathed deeply of the salty fragrance of the ocean, entranced by the music and the beauty around her, she felt completely at peace, and her heartache dimmed almost to nonexistence. She couldn't explain why, but in Luke's presence she felt safe. She sensed a kindred spirit. There seemed to be a great sadness about him, a longing and loneliness beyond the loss of his wife. Maybe it was a sadness resulting from the childhood he had alluded to, a sadness similar to her own, a sadness that caused him to hold most of the people who'd come into his life at arm's length. How else could she explain the bond that she—and apparently he—so immediately felt?

She closed her eyes, lulled into serenity by Luke's beautiful music, and drifted off to sleep with her hand nestled in Sitka's luxurious fur.

<h1 style="text-align:center">Chapter Five</h1>

Softly playing his guitar, Luke watched Dana fall asleep. She was the first woman he'd invited aboard the *Warm Breeze* since Jamie had died. Sitka wasn't the only one who thought he'd found someone special. Luke turned his attention to the night sky, running through the song, about unfulfilled dreams—and new beginnings—again and again. He improvised a few notes and fine-tuned the lyrics and felt more satisfied with it than he had when he'd started.

A brief burst of fireworks, set off from a neighboring boat and no doubt left over from the Fourth of July, popped in accompaniment, and Luke watched their colors blossom. He heard Dana stir—was that a whimper? He looked down at her, but she was quiet.

Luke set aside his guitar. "What do you think, Sitka? Will she get too chilly lying there? Think I should wake her up to go below?"

At the sound of his name, Sitka stood up and stretched. Luke gently touched Dana's shoulder, barely resisting the impulse to take her in his arms. She stirred, her eyes fluttering open. "I should go," she murmured.

"Why don't you stay?" Luke whispered. "You can have the berth, and I'll sleep in the salon."

When Dana nodded in response, Luke helped her to her feet and then guided her down the steps and to the forward cabin, where he helped her onto his V-berth. He covered her with a light wool blanket, and Sitka lay down protectively beside the bunk.

Luke blew out the overhead lantern and stretched out on one of the salon seats, his long legs dangling over the end. Though he tried to doze, he couldn't stop thinking about Dana.

"I give up," he finally said and sat up.

At the sound of his master's voice Sitka came out and walked over to Luke, rubbing against his leg.

"Giving up your post, eh, boy? Yeah, I like her too. A lot," Luke whispered. "Haven't found out much about her, though." Luke rubbed his eyes and then stood up and ran his fingers through his hair. "Might as well have some coffee."

He rummaged through the cupboard and grabbed the coffee tin. Though he'd replaced the beans in it countless times since Jamie's death, he'd left the handwritten note she'd pasted across the front of the canister: *Jamie's favorite. There'd better be some left!* He kept buying her favorite blend.

With a heavy sigh, he set the tin down on the counter and then pulled out his wallet and removed the photograph of Jamie. He had taken it on the island, and it was his favorite. She was sitting on the natural rocky arch they had referred to as the rock bridge, and he had captured her radiant smile. He could almost hear her infectious laugh. Luke crouched and scratched Sitka's ears. "You never knew her, Sitka. You would have loved her. Just like you love Dana."

Luke stared at Jamie's photograph, remembering one of the last things she'd said to him. "I know you'll eventually meet someone else. Don't feel guilty about it." Ignoring Luke's protestations, she had weakly squeezed his hand and insisted, "I don't want you to spend the rest of your life alone. You have too much to offer another very lucky woman."

Overcome with emotion, Luke carefully returned Jamie's picture to his wallet. Suddenly, despite Jamie's words and his growing attraction to Dana, he felt uncomfortable with another woman sleeping in the cabin. For the first time in a long time he asked himself why Jamie had had to die.

Luke's reverie was interrupted by Sitka's persistent whining. "What is it, boy?"

Sitka began tugging on Luke's right pant leg, pulling him toward the forward cabin. Quickly following, Luke found Dana sleeping fitfully, moaning and tossing and turning. Suddenly she let out a small cry and threw off the blanket.

Luke leaned over and gently replaced the blanket, accidentally brushing Dana's shoulder as he did so. Her eyes popped open, and a look of fear spread across her face. Screaming in terror, she beat his chest with her fists as if to fight him off.

Swiftly and decisively, Luke took Dana in his arms, holding her gently and stroking her hair. He whispered what he hoped were soothing words, anxious to ease her distress. His actions had the desired effect, for her screams subsided and she leaned against him, her body drenched with sweat. The screams gave way to sobs, which little by little diminished into whimpering. Eventually the crying stopped entirely, and Dana relaxed in Luke's arms. Luke knew what it was like to hurt, and Dana was definitely hurting. He cradled her for a long time, rocking her back and forth. Sitka paced in the main cabin, and as Dana's breathing finally became regular and slow, he placed his paw on Luke's knee, nuzzling her.

"I think she'll be okay now, Sitka," Luke said as he laid her on the berth and covered her with the blanket. She immediately curled into a fetal position, clutching the blanket to her chin like a small child, and slept peacefully. Luke bent over and brushed his lips against her cheek, tasting the salt on her skin, the dried tears the only evidence of her nightmare.

It was just past 7:00 a.m., and Luke was up on deck, varnishing one of the teak hatch covers. He replayed the events of the night before and wondered whether Dana's nightmare had been an isolated incident or if such dreams were a regular feature in her life. He glanced over at Sitka, lying in the stern, soaking up the morning sun. How attuned Sitka had been to Dana!

Just then Luke heard her stirring below. He looked down through the open hatch, watching as she headed toward the companionway, climbed a couple of treads, and then abruptly stopped. He figured she was trying to compose herself before facing him. Well, he wasn't about to make it harder on her by asking questions about the night before. Besides, what would she say? *That was one helluva nightmare, wasn't it? Sorry, but you got more than you bargained for when you invited me to dinner.*

The footfalls began again, and Dana soon emerged through the hatchway onto the deck.

"Good morning," Luke said with a welcoming smile. "Beautiful day. Not a cloud in the sky." *That sounded lame,* he thought.

"Yes, it is glorious," Dana said, also too brightly, greeting Sitka with a hug.

Luke cleared his throat. "I make a pretty good garden scramble. I throw in about everything I can find in the fridge."

Dana shook her head as she pulled on her boots. "Thanks, but I don't have much of an appetite." She smiled at him gratefully, though Luke wasn't sure whether it was for the offer of breakfast or for not bringing up the events of last night.

"Are you sure?" He set his brush across the can of varnish and stood up. "No trouble at all."

"I'm sure. Besides, I really have to go."

"Okay," Luke said, helping Dana step off the boat. "Let's make that a rain check."

Sitka had already jumped out of the boat and was heading down the dock. Luke whistled for him, and he ran back, stopping at Dana's side.

"I'm sorry, Sitka." Dana scratched his ears. "You need to stay." Turning to Luke she said, "Thanks for a lovely dinner. I had a lot of fun. I haven't laughed that much in a long time."

"I had fun too. Listen, Dana…" Luke wanted to prolong her departure. More than that, he really wanted to see her again. "I was wondering…see that mountain over there, the one that looks like a chocolate drop?" He pointed across the bay. "What would you say about a hike to the top? The view is really something. It's actually a fairly easy climb, though it is steep in places, so I think I'd leave Sitka with Jake."

When Dana didn't reply, Luke continued, "We can even swing by a bird rookery on the way over."

Dana studied the mountain. "Well, I *have* been hoping to photograph some puffins," she finally said.

"Puffins I can show you. Guaranteed. Can you meet me here in a couple of hours?" He hoped her resolve would last that long.

Dana was still gazing across the bay. Before Luke could ask again, she turned to him and nodded slowly.

Luke nodded back. "Good. We'll need a high tide to enter the lagoon where we anchor the boat, and the tide will be just about right then."

As soon as Dana got back to her room at the inn, she opened her laptop and addressed an email to Mark. And then her fingers froze as the cursor blinked steadily over the blank message box.

She wanted to write him, but she had no idea what to say—especially since her last email had been so short. And especially after a night like she'd just had.

> *Hi! Long time, no talk. Things here are great—slept over at a new friend's house last night after he fed me a beautiful dinner and opened up about his dead wife and his troubled childhood. Doesn't that sound familiar, maybe like a certain Dana you know? Yeah, I really do feel super comfortable with him—and with his dog, who reminds me of all the important dogs in my life. But we're just friends! Swear!*

Dana's shoulders slumped. Her fingers remained still.

> *Mark. Had another nightmare last night. It was horrible, absolutely horrible. I don't know what set me off, because I'd been doing so well! Maybe it was the fireworks—I sort of remember fireworks, and they sound like gunshots, of course, so...anyway, I'm exhausted today. But I'm still going to go on a hike up a mountain. And I feel better than I have in a long time. I'm letting the scenery calm me. I'm making new friends, who seem to understand my pain, calm me.*

Dana banged shut the laptop, the email remaining blank and unsent.

As much as she felt guilty not being able to communicate with Mark, she also didn't want to cancel on Luke. She stood and stripped off her outfit from the day before. Dinner had been just dinner, and this hike would be just a hike. She was feeling so good. She started unfolding hiking clothes she hadn't yet worn. A piece of paper fluttered out from the shirt.

Dana—I don't know how long it will take for you to find this note, but know that whenever it is, I'm thinking of you. I'm proud of you. I hope you're not alone all the time and are around people sometimes, even if you don't want to talk to them.

Dana held Mark's note for a few long minutes. It felt alive with concern. She was grateful for Mark's love; she really was. But instead of tucking the note into her bag or setting it on her nightstand, she folded it into a tiny square and set it in the garbage can. She couldn't quite put her finger on why the note rubbed her the wrong way, but it did. *Be around people? I'm going to climb a mountain.*

The *Warm Breeze* cut through the waves easily. As Luke sailed the boat, he studied Dana. She seemed like a different person than the one he'd said good-bye to just a few hours earlier. Then she had been quiet and withdrawn, appearing as vulnerable as a child. He had felt very protective of her and had been more than a little worried about her. Now she was radiant, standing on the bow of the boat with her face into the wind, laughing and obviously thoroughly enjoying herself. And obviously thoroughly capable of caring for herself. She didn't need a protector, he realized, even when she appeared vulnerable.

Speaking of which, what hellish nightmare had caused her to react as she had? And why was she alone in Alaska? Was she running away from something—or someone? Was someone searching for her? Or was she perhaps searching for something herself? He gave up asking unanswerable questions and instead focused on the day at hand.

As Luke had promised Dana, he first sailed toward the island seabird rookery. The raucous din created by the summer residents could be heard a quarter of a mile away. The noise became almost deafening as he steered the *Warm Breeze* in close under power while Dana took photograph after photograph of puffins, murres, seagulls, and cormorants. Once she was satisfied with her photographs and they were once again under sail, Luke continued tacking across the bay and headed into the lagoon that would be their jumping-off point for the hike. After dropping anchor, Luke unhooked the lightweight, inflatable dinghy from its berth atop the cabin and lowered it over the side. He rowed the few yards to shore, where he then beached the small tender.

The hike to the peak of the chocolate-drop mountain wasn't strenuous, but it was long. Luke reached the summit first and helped Dana scramble up the loose shale near the top. He moved to one side so she could have the full effect of the sweeping panorama.

"Wow! You were right!" Dana set down her pack and retrieved her camera. "This is spectacular. How high are we?"

"About twenty-five hundred feet."

One side of the weathered peak looked straight into a glacial valley dotted with small lakes. The other side commanded a dramatic view of the entire bay, including the town and three volcanoes.

Dana took photos till her trigger finger ached and then sat down beside Luke in the exact center of the flattened summit. "Any of that trail mix left?"

"Plenty." Luke handed her the bag. He pointed. "Jamie and I once climbed that cone-shaped volcano on the left."

"You're kidding!"

"Nope. We took some scientist friends of ours over there to

study the volcano soon after an eruption. We figured as long as we were there, we might as well climb it."

Luke offered Dana a bottle of water, and she took a long drink.

"What was it like?" she asked.

"I remember huge pumice and lava blocks sitting on top of the alders at the base. Some of the lava bombs—they're rocks hurled out of the volcano—were as big as cars. Live plants were nearly buried in ash but still surviving." Luke stretched out on the rocky outcropping. "The climbing was easier as we approached the top, but we stopped before we reached the summit. Couldn't see anything. Might as well have been walking through a steam kettle. The ash was very warm. In fact, if you dug into it about six inches, it was too hot to touch."

"Weren't you worried it would erupt again?"

"Didn't think about it. The scientists were monitoring the seismic activity, so I guess we figured as long as they were there, it was okay for us to be there too."

"I've never met anyone who's climbed a volcano before."

Luke cocked an eyebrow and waved his arm, encompassing the magnificent scenery. "Stay here a while, and who knows what you might end up doing!"

"Well, I don't know about climbing a volcano, but this is wonderful," Dana said. She pulled off her sweatshirt. "It's so beautiful up here. And peaceful. Nothing but the sound of the wind."

"That it is," Luke agreed. He couldn't resist reaching over and touching one of Dana's braids. "Your hair is beautiful."

Dana smiled shyly. "Thanks. My best feature."

"I don't know about that."

"When I was a little girl, strangers would stop my mom and comment about the color."

"I'll bet you were really cute."

"I don't think about my childhood."

Luke noticed the sadness that washed over her face. Had she lost her parents when she was young?

"May I ask you a question?" Dana asked.

Luke nodded. "You can ask me anything you want."

"I know this must be hard for you to talk about." Dana's voice was soft and caring. "But I'm wondering how you were able to forget that awful time when your wife died. How did you put it all behind you and move on?"

Sometimes I'm not sure I have. Luke sat up and adjusted his baseball cap, staring at the volcano and thinking about her question. And was it as much about Dana as it was about him? After several seconds he said, "First of all, you never forget." He kept his voice calm. "You try to accept what's happened. You stop asking why. If you can do that, hopefully you can let go and find an inner peace."

He stole a quick sideways glance at Dana. "Living on the island helped me. I needed to be alone with my grief. It's not like I didn't appreciate others' concern, but my way of working through something is to be by myself. Listening to the water break on the rocks, the wind sighing through the trees. Sometimes it seemed as if the trees were crying too."

Dana touched Luke's arm. He curved his hand around her fingers and squeezed them gently, grateful for her caring touch.

"One day I stopped thinking about why I was hurting so much," he continued, "and started focusing on the little things that helped me to feel happy." He gazed across the expansive scenery. "Like being with Sitka, watching a sunset, playing my guitar. Or enjoying the taste of a just-brewed cup of coffee or halibut so fresh it's practically still flopping. And feeling the wind on my face while sailing the *Warm Breeze*." Luke turned and cupped Dana's face in his palm, fighting the urge to kiss her. "Or enjoying the company of an intriguing and very beautiful woman."

Dana pulled away. "Luke, I need to tell you…I should have told you before…"

Was she going to tell him about her nightmare?

"I'm involved with someone."

"Oh!" Stunned, Luke didn't know what to say or think. That was *not* what he had expected.

"He wants to get married."

"Do you?" Luke's voice was almost a whisper.

"I'm not…" Dana stared out at the vast panorama. "Yes. If I can only…"

Luke was surprised by how much this disclosure disturbed him and tried to find some hope in her hesitant answer. He turned away from her, wanting to conceal the disappointment that spread across his face.

"Mark's a wonderful man," Dana said, still looking into the distance. "He's kind, loving, devoted, gentle, and understanding. And very, very patient. But…"

She sighed and fell silent. Luke waited for her to continue her unfinished thought.

"One of the reasons I came to Alaska was to think about our relationship. The problem is…" Dana sighed again and stood up. She took several steps toward the bay, seemingly oblivious to the steep drop-off that was just a few feet away. Luke jumped up, fearful she might lose her footing as she approached the precipice. He was reaching out to grab her when she stopped, inches short of the edge.

Dana spoke so softly Luke almost didn't hear her next words. "We all have a past, don't we?"

As if by unspoken agreement, they dropped the subject of Dana's relationship with Mark. They went back to enjoying the view, uncomplicated conversation, and a hearty lunch. Soon after eating, they started back down the mountain. It was evening by the time they returned to the base of the mountain and then got back onboard the *Warm Breeze* and set sail across the bay for town. Approaching the harbor, Luke took down the sails and started up the engine: he maneuvered the sailboat through the harbor channel and into its berth.

Though he had tried to resist wondering about Dana's nightmare, Luke had been thinking about how troubled she seemed and how much he wanted to help her, if he could.

Well, there was one thing he could offer. When he had secured the lines, he turned to her and took her hands in his. "Listen, I'm going back to the island tomorrow morning, and I'd love for you to come." Dana immediately started to protest, but he clasped her hands tighter and explained, "When Jamie died, I decided to continue pursuing the dreams we shared. Focusing on these things has helped me to continue living and also to feel that the sacrifices she made for us while I was away fishing so much of the time weren't in vain—that in some way she continues to live on through those dreams. One was to build what was to be our dream house on the island. It's pretty much done now, and I know Jamie would have loved it. I know *you* would love it."

Dana shook her head. "Thank you for asking…but I can't."

Luke persisted. "Look, I understand that you're involved with someone, and I respect that—and you. It's just that, not that I mean to pry or anything…well, the island is the most healing place I know. You're welcome to come for as long as you want. Or just for a day. I'm between carpentry jobs now, so I'll be around."

"No, really, I can't. But I appreciate the offer. It means a lot to me." Dana stepped off the boat. "I've had a wonderful time, Luke. Thank you again."

"The pleasure has been all mine, let me assure you."

At the end of the dock, she turned to wave. "Hug Sitka good-bye for me."

Even though the possibility of a romantic relationship was now out of the question, Luke wasn't ready to say good-bye to Dana or sever their connection, or give up trying to help. He called out to her, "Sitka would be disappointed if he didn't see you again. I think he's ready to jump ship and go home with you. So if you change your mind about coming to the island, find someone to bring you over. Everyone knows where it is."

Chapter Six

ONE DAY PASSED, THEN TWO, THEN THREE. SLEEP AGAIN ELUDED Dana, and she spent most of her time roaming the beach. She often found herself checking the slip where the *Warm Breeze* had been docked—just in case. Just as often, she thought about that night—had it only been a few days ago?—when she'd had dinner on Luke's boat. She could still feel his strong arms around her during her nightmare. Undaunted by her panic, he didn't seem to care that she was hitting him and screaming. And she couldn't stop thinking about the little touches they'd shared during the hike up the chocolate drop.

What was it about this man she hardly knew yet felt like she had known her whole life? They were connected in a way she couldn't explain and had never experienced before, not even with Mark. She felt strong when she was with him. And his offer of a healing place kept coming back to her.

She thought about how her business partner had responded when Dana told her she didn't know how long she'd be gone. Using her favorite expression, Andrea had assured her, "Not to worry. Take as long as you need. And Mark will understand too. Your happiness is his primary concern. But I don't need to tell *you* that."

No, Dana didn't need reminding how much Mark adored her. And in return, *she* couldn't stop thinking about another man. She looked out her window and saw the mountain they had climbed. Was Luke in her life for a reason? The truth was, she felt compelled to go to his island and see him again.

"No strings attached," Luke had said.

She decided to go.

After packing her belongings, Dana sat down at the small table by the window in her room to write a note to Mark. *Dear Mark…*she began the email. And the cursor didn't move any farther. She picked up her phone to call him. A commercial airline pilot, he should be home from his flight to Atlanta by now, if his schedule hadn't changed.

For some reason she thought back to the time she was remodeling her bed-and-breakfast and Lucky had come running into the yard with her muzzle full of porcupine quills. While Dana tried to comfort her and get her into the car to take her to the vet, Mark found some vinegar in her makeshift kitchen. He expertly applied it to Lucky's nose and mouth to deaden the pain and carefully removed the quills.

Oh, Mark. Kind, gentle, loving Mark. Do you really think we could be happy together? I know you keep telling me my past doesn't matter, but…how could you possibly handle it if I told you everything?

Dana dialed Mark's number. She had to admit she was relieved when his voice mail picked up. A message was easier. "Mark, I'm going to a place near here without phone, Internet, or mail service, so I'll contact you again when I can. I'm confident I'll figure things out. I love you."

Part Two

Chapter Seven

From her seat in the twenty-two-foot aluminum skiff, Dana could see Sitka react when he heard the whine of the outboard motor approaching the island. He yipped wildly as he ran to the edge of the mossy cliff.

Dana's heart jumped at the sight of Luke, who had responded to Sitka's vocalizations and followed him to the overlook above the rocky point that served as a dock. Luke and Sitka were waiting at the water's edge when the boat pulled up.

"I hope your invitation still stands," Dana said, shouting to be heard over Sitka's enthusiastic barking as the captain, a young woman named Susan, deftly maneuvered the skiff into a cleft in the rocky shoreline.

"Absolutely." Luke's smile was genuine and welcoming. "And Sitka's sure happy to see you. He rarely barks or makes a sound other than an occasional *woof* or *woo-woo*. Hand me your gear." He steadied the boat with one hand while holding the other out to her.

Dana tried not to let her nervousness show as she handed over her duffel bag and then took Luke's hand to climb out of the skiff. She had barely set both feet on land when Sitka jumped up on her, almost knocking her over in his exuberance to see her. "I'm glad to see you too, Sitka!" Dana hugged him tightly, relieved at the distraction. She then turned to Susan. "Thanks for bringing me over."

"Anytime," Susan replied. She pulled a packet from under the skiff's console and held it out. "Here's your mail, Luke. Oh, and Jake sent this over." She reached for a covered storage container and handed it to Luke. "His latest fiddlehead creation. Some kind of marinated salad."

"Can't wait to try it. Thanks." Luke pushed Susan's boat away from the rocks. "Tell Jake I won't be in town this week."

"Will do." Susan waved as she thrust the engine's controls into forward gear.

Luke raised the salad to Dana. "Guess we have our veggies taken care of for dinner." He then made an exaggerated bow. "This way, if you please, miss."

"Thank you," Dana replied, with a nervous laugh. To ease her apprehension about whether she had made the right decision in coming to Luke's island, she purposefully focused on her surroundings. The set of stairs they were climbing led to a large cedar deck that bordered the front of the house and wrapped partially around each side. The land had been cleared just enough to allow for the house to get plenty of sun yet retain a sense of being a part of its surroundings. The structure itself was stained a weathered gray that from a distance blended in with the trees. Large windows covered the facade, which let in maximum light as well as the gorgeous views. And flower boxes were mounted in every conceivable spot along the deck railings and below the windows, the multitude of colorful blooms seeming even brighter in the brilliant afternoon sun. "Luke, your home is beautiful," Dana said. "And these flowers! I wish I had your green thumb."

"Jake's the one with the green thumb, not me. Every year we spend a day planting flowers he's grown in his greenhouse. All I do is water them."

"Does he have a big greenhouse?"

"He does. He's even managed to grow a couple of fruit trees in it."

Dana noticed a redwood hot tub in one corner of the deck. She glanced uncomfortably at Luke. "I don't have a bathing suit."

"Oops, sorry I forgot to mention the hot tub. But don't worry. I'm sure we can come up with something for you to wear." Luke smiled reassuringly as he took Dana's elbow. "I'll show you the inside first, and then we can take a hike around the island, if you'd like."

Dana's discomfort eased. "That would be great." She crossed the threshold, looking around the spacious main floor. Her gaze stopped at the antique upright. "A piano! How wonderful."

"Do you play?"

"A little," she said, eager to run her fingers over the keys.

Everything was constructed of wood. The ceiling was pine, the floor oak. Sunlight streaming through the windows highlighted the cedar walls. The dormant volcano Luke had pointed out from the chocolate-drop mountain was visible from the kitchen's bay window.

They climbed the spiral staircase that connected the four levels. The staircase was in a tower that had four large octagonal windows on each floor.

Dana's eyes widened. "I've never seen so many windows in one house. I feel like I'm in the trees." The tranquility permeating Luke's home enveloped Dana like a cocoon.

When they reached the small room at the top of the tower, Dana said, "Wow, this really is like a tree house. The view is breathtaking."

"This can be your room," Luke said.

Dana turned in a circle, drinking in the scenery. "Thank you!

I love it! It's like something from a fairy tale, like being in a castle turret."

Luke smiled at her enthusiasm.

Dana stepped outside onto the deck that surrounded the room. "You even have flower boxes up here." She leaned against the railing, sighing with contentment. "Oh, Luke, this is so wonderful. I can't thank you enough for inviting me." A thought struck her. "How did you get all this over here? Did you hire a barge?"

Luke laughed. "Nope. Bit by bit. Seems like more often than not we arrived at low tide and had to carry the loads up the rocks. Except for the piano. That was brought over by helicopter."

"Helicopter?!"

"Yeah. The locals are still talking about it." He put down Dana's duffel bag. "Let's take that walk. I'd like to show you the rock bridge."

"I can't wait. Let me dig out my tennis shoes, and I'll be ready to go."

Sitka led the way. A narrow trail wound around the island's perimeter through lush, almost jungle-like vegetation. Tall, densely spaced spruce trees covered the nine-acre island. Shafts of sunlight pierced the tree branches, creating a patchwork of light on the ferns and devil's club that covered the forest floor. Blueberry bushes were everywhere. The thick woods muted all sounds except for the persistent slapping of the waves against the shore. The air smelled of the morning rain and decaying earth.

They finally reached the rock bridge, and Dana's eyes opened wide at the sight. About twenty yards offshore was a small "satellite" island, which was connected to the main island by a dramatic rock arch. At midrange and higher tides, the rocky beach beneath the arch was submerged, completing the bridge effect. Both the natural bridge and the small island were lushly covered with moss, while blueberry bushes and small trees thrived in the unobstructed sunlight. On the mossy point, Dana and Luke leaned against a rotting spruce log and relaxed in the warm sun. Luke's house at the far end of the island was just visible across the water from this vantage point. Sitka plopped down beside Dana, his head at her feet, and promptly fell asleep. Dana was quietly content, feeling no need to speak. Luke apparently felt likewise, for he too said nothing. The only sounds were the water lapping against the rocks and an occasional birdsong.

After several minutes Luke broke the silence. "We're glad you came."

"So am I." Dana scratched Sitka's stomach and spread her fingers through his thick fur.

She turned to face Luke. It was evident from his expression just how happy he was to see her. She got the impression he was about to take her in his arms—and she had to admit to herself, she wasn't sure she would object. But as if to ensure he would maintain his distance, Luke quickly stood up and put his hands in his pockets.

He cleared his throat slightly and then explained, "This place has special meaning for me. Kind of an island within an island, where you know it's just you and your thoughts." Luke gazed across the water. "After Jamie died, I came here every day at sunrise and sunset. This is the place I allowed myself to think about her, cry about what we would never have, and feel sorry for myself."

Dana could feel his heartache as she waited for him to continue.

"Slowly I started thinking about why I missed her so much, and my sorrow evolved into a celebration of her life and the few years we had together. I was finally able to let go of the pain and focus on the joy."

Touched by Luke's sharing of such private feelings, Dana felt words of her own well up inside her, but she kept them to herself.

Luke shifted gears by pointing to a blueberry bush behind her and saying, "These blueberries will be ripe any day. Hope you'll be here long enough to enjoy some of my famous blueberry pancakes." He offered his hand to Dana. "Right now, though, I hope you like shrimp. I pulled my pots just before you got here."

"I love shrimp," Dana said, taking his hand and getting to her feet. "As a matter of fact, it's my favorite food."

"Well, you're in for a real treat. You won't get them any fresher than this. And Jake's salad will no doubt go perfectly with them."

They headed back across the rock bridge, Sitka once again in the lead, and walked back to the house via a sheltered cove with a small beach. Dana periodically stopped to claim some treasure that had washed up on shore—a shell here, a piece of beach glass there. To keep the conversation light, she asked, "Do you know there's a kind of deep-sea shrimp that emits a blue light to temporarily blind its enemies?"

Luke smiled broadly. "As a matter of fact, I do. Can't remember its name, though."

"*Acanthephyra purpurea.*"

He looked over at her. "I'm impressed. Okay, here's one for you. Do you know what a devilfish is?"

"Well, in fact, it's a couple of different species," Dana answered. "Both manta rays and octopus are known by that name. Supposedly in the early sixteen hundreds a gigantic octopus grabbed two sailors while they were scraping the hull of their ship."

"Never knew that. Do you know why it's unlucky to kill a seagull?"

"The souls of sailors lost at sea live on in seagulls."

They approached the boardwalk leading back to the house, and Luke smiled appreciatively. "So, where did you come by all these tidbits of sea lore?" he asked.

"I grew up in Seattle, and the ocean was part of my life. In fact, from our house you could see the ferries and ships coming and going." She sighed. "I used to daydream about stowing away."

"A stowaway, huh? That would have been an adventure."

Dana shrugged. "I wasn't looking for an adventure. I was looking for an escape."

Luke gave her a what-do-you-mean-by-that expression, but before he could ask, Dana continued. "Anyway, I read a lot."

It was obvious Luke knew Dana wanted to avoid the subject when he said, "Well, I can see I've met my match. Ready for some shrimp?"

Dana nodded. "Being on the water always makes me hungry. What can I do to help?"

Luke handed her the bucket that was sitting outside the front door. "This is sea water we'll use to boil the shrimp. Why don't you start heating it in the large pot that's in the cabinet next to the fridge. I'll throw more wood in the hot tub stove. I need to stoke the fire several times a day to keep the water warm."

"Okay," Dana replied. "I'm not much of a cook, but boiling water I can handle."

Luke stoked the wood-burning stove that heated the hot tub. Then he showed Dana how to cook the shrimp to perfection, scooping them out of the boiling water as soon as they floated. They sat down at the table with a huge pile of shrimp in front of them and plenty of cocktail sauce. Luke expertly demonstrated how he liked to break off the heads, pinch the base of the tail, and pull out the meat in one smooth motion.

Dana followed his lead. "Yum. These are delicious." She reached for another handful. "I've never tasted shrimp so sweet."

"Thought you'd like 'em. I was lucky today. Not like yesterday, when the starfish got to the bait first."

"Starfish are beautiful, but they do live up to their reputation as the walking stomachs of the sea."

Luke jumped up and grabbed Jake's salad and a couple of small plates. "Almost forgot this in our shrimp-feeding frenzy."

Their conversation for the rest of the meal mostly consisted of a series of umms and yums. When they had pretty much finished everything on the table, Luke asked, "Can I get you anything else?"

Dana groaned. "No thanks. I'm beyond full." She pushed back from the table and studied the house. "Your home has so many interesting angles and different shapes to the windows. I could have used your imagination when I was working on my place."

Luke looked at Dana with interest.

"About five years ago I inherited my grandparents' house on the Oregon coast. I quit my job in Seattle and decided to renovate the house into a bed-and-breakfast. My happiest times as a child were the summers I spent there." A small sigh escaped Dana's lips as she played with the ends of her braids, separating the tangled curls.

"I've known Mark my whole life. He lived next door to my grandparents. I'm a couple of years younger than he is, and I used to follow him around like a puppy. He never seemed to mind, even though his brothers kidded him. I told Mark everything—well, almost everything—when I was growing up. Our relationship kind of evolved over the years, and I was out of college and working when we realized we loved each other in a romantic way, not just as friends. He had become an airline pilot; he was based in Seattle at the time. He's now based in Portland."

Dana got up from the table and walked out onto the deck. She knew it was increasingly obvious that something painful was troubling her. But she also knew, instinctively, Luke wouldn't ask her about it or expect her to talk to him until she was ready. Would she ever be? She honestly didn't know.

Luke followed Dana outside. When he spoke, his voice was gentle and full of concern. "Guess I'd better check the hot tub. Are you up for a soak?"

Turning toward Luke, Dana dabbed at the corners of her eyes and nodded.

"Good. Me too. The water should be just about right." He walked over to the corner of the deck and checked the water temperature with a floating thermometer. "Yep. Perfect. By the way, have you ever been to Disney World?"

"No…"

"Well," Luke called as he stepped into the house. Dana heard a cabinet open and shut, and Luke returned with an armload of towels. "Allow me to transport you there through"—he held each towel up so Dana could see them—"Goofy or Donald Duck, your choice."

Smiling, Dana took Goofy from Luke's outstretched hand and said, "Goofy, of course. You know how I love dogs."

"One of the first people I met in Alaska, a fisherman named Sam, wanted to take Brian, his ten-year-old grandson, to Disney World one Christmas. He asked me to go with him so I could help entertain Brian." Luke grinned. "I'm not sure who had more fun, Brian or me. Didn't get to do stuff like that when I was a kid. I brought these towels home as a souvenir.

"Okay, that's step one." He motioned for her to follow him up the stairs to his loft bedroom. "I have a pair of Mickey Mouse boxer shorts that Brian gave me that Christmas," Luke said. "Never been worn. They should do for the bottom half of a bathing suit."

"Okay by me," Dana said.

"They've got to be here somewhere." Luke rummaged through several drawers. "Aha!" Triumphantly he held up the boxer shorts still wrapped in their packaging. "Here you are, mademoiselle."

"Thank you, kind sir," Dana said with a smile.

"Now for the top...I just happen to have a T-shirt that matches." Luke continued rummaging through another drawer until he held up the colorful shirt and gave it to her. "I'll meet you downstairs after you've changed."

Dana climbed the steep stairs to her tower room, thinking yet again how easily Luke put her at ease and distanced her from her troubled thoughts. She quickly changed, and when she descended with Goofy wrapped securely around her body and walked out onto the deck, she felt relaxed and calm. Luke was already soaking in the inviting water.

Dana slipped off the towel, climbed into the tub, and sank onto the bench opposite Luke, the water coming up to her neck. "Ahhhh, this is wonderful! You're right. The temperature's perfect."

"Some people don't like the water a degree less than one hundred and four. I prefer it between ninety-eight and one hundred because at that temperature, you can soak in the water for hours."

"Isn't it hard to regulate the temperature when you heat with wood?" Dana asked.

Luke draped his muscular arms on the edge of the hot tub. "After months of painstaking trial and error, I finally stumbled upon the solution. Once the temperature reaches ninety-six degrees, you throw in one more load of wood, have a beer, and sit back and relax. It heats up fast at that temperature."

Dana laughed.

Luke continued, "Of course, you have to factor in a few things, such as air temperature, wind speed and direction, and precipitation, not to mention the number of soakers."

Dana nodded earnestly. Then she smiled. "Oh, Luke, I'm really enjoying myself. Thank you so much for inviting me." She turned in a circle, soaking up the view as well as the heat from the water. "The scenery is so beautiful, and being here is more peaceful than I could have imagined. Any troubles just seem to fade away."

Luke returned Dana's smile. "As advertised, the most healing place I know."

They soaked in comfortable silence for a long time as the hot, soothing water relaxed them. After a while Luke asked, "Mind if I play the guitar?"

"Not at all! That would be wonderful." Dana leaned her head against the side of the tub and sighed contentedly.

Luke stood up and climbed out of the hot tub, tying the Donald Duck towel around his waist. He retrieved his guitar and then sat on the bench that partially surrounded the hot tub. "Here's a new song I've been working on. Hope you like it."

Dana closed her eyes. As she listened to Luke play, she once again marveled at his ability to create music that connected with the ache in her heart and eased her pain.

Luke played several more songs, and by the time he set down his guitar, the sun was setting behind the volcano. "I'd better get out," Dana said. "I'm shriveled up like a prune."

"I'll go get your bed ready."

"Thanks." Dana sighed with contentment as she stepped out of the hot tub, wrapping her beach towel securely around her upper body. "I think I'll have to get a hot tub for my B and B. This has been wonderful."

Luke smiled in agreement and then headed for the tower stairs.

The inside of the house was warm and inviting. Dana took her time following Luke up the stairs, stopping at each level to savor the beauty of the island through the octagonal windows.

"I hope these cushions from my old fishing boat will be okay," Luke said as Dana reached the top step. "I don't have many visitors, and I haven't thought much about furniture."

Dana flopped down on the foam cushions and nodded. "Very comfy."

"I'll get some sheets and blankets. And a pillow."

Dana was outside on the tower-room deck taking pictures and enjoying the last of the sunset when Luke returned with the bedclothes. Sitka followed, carrying a threadbare stuffed animal in his mouth.

"Sitka!" Dana cried. She entered the room and carefully took the worn brown bear from Sitka's mouth. "Sorry, boy, but you can't have this. It's very special to me."

"Sorry," Luke said. "Guess it must have fallen out of your duffel bag."

"It's okay. Doesn't look like there's any harm done." She patted Sitka's head to reassure him.

"Is there anything else you need?"

"No, I'm fine," Dana said. She touched his arm lightly. "Thanks."

"Well, okay, then. I'll be one level down if you need me."

Sitka was turning around and around, trying to find a

comfortable spot in the small space that remained after setting up Dana's bed. "Sorry, boy," Luke said to Sitka. "Not much room for you up here. You're going to have to sleep downstairs in your usual spot."

"Luke…" Dana began. Then she shook her head. "Actually, I don't know what I want to say," she continued awkwardly. "Being here…it's the first time I have felt at peace in many years. Thank you." Impulsively she gave Luke a quick hug. "Good night."

"Night, Dana," Luke said and turned to lead Sitka down the stairs. "Sweet dreams."

The brief night was already fading with the approaching dawn as Luke tossed and turned, unable to sleep. He couldn't stop thinking about Dana. He glanced toward the staircase and noticed Sitka was not sleeping next to the bed. He got up, threw on a pair of well-worn sweatpants, and quietly walked up the spiral staircase.

As Luke reached the top step he saw, as expected, Sitka sleeping curled up near Dana's head. Obviously Sitka missed Dana too. Feeling uncomfortable peeking in on her this way, Luke started to turn around and head back down the stairs when he noticed the fruits of Dana's beachcombing carefully placed on two of the window ledges: a large clamshell, a piece of twisted and dried seaweed, a shard of beach glass, a delicate and perfectly formed scallop shell, a triton, and two limpets. Several other shells he didn't know the names of completed the display.

Dana had also placed a framed photograph on the windowsill nearest the head of her bed, and his heart warmed when he saw it was a snapshot of Sitka sprawled on the rocks below his home. At the same time that he found it sweet that Dana had honored Sitka this way, he wondered why she hadn't set out a picture of Mark. She must love him—otherwise she wouldn't be considering marrying him. And why was the decision so difficult? When he had fallen in love with Jamie, he had known with certainty he wanted to spend the rest of his life with her.

The rustling of Dana's bedclothes as she shifted position drew Luke's attention to her. She was sleeping on her side, her arms wrapped tightly around her stuffed animal. He remembered how she had clutched the ragged bear to her breast after she had carefully removed it from Sitka's mouth, almost as if it were a lifeline.

Luke looked at her thoughtfully. Her face was vulnerable in the early-morning light. Her hair, a tangle of ringlets, was spread on the pillow like an exotic fan. He was glad her hair was free from the braids she always seemed to wear. He wished he could bury his face in the mass of curls and inhale the delicate rose scent that wafted up to him.

One of her legs was entwined in the down comforter. It dawned on him then that she seemed to always wear baggy clothes, which effectively concealed her shapely body. He carefully reached down and untangled her leg. Tenderly readjusting the comforter, he whispered, "Why is it I feel as if I've known you a lifetime instead of just a few days? And why, dammit, do you have to have a boyfriend?"

He put the gun to her head. She screamed, her fists hammering against his chest. She screamed again, but still no one came to her rescue.

He shoved her favorite pair of socks in her mouth to shut her up and then held her arms against her sides to control her. But she fought even harder, kicking him repeatedly until he hit her with the butt of the gun. She crumpled to the floor.

Dana awoke from her nightmare sweating and breathing raggedly. Scared and disoriented, she stared at the skylights in the circular ceiling, and just as she remembered with relief where she was, Sitka licked her face, calming her further. She smiled at how Sitka had returned to her room in the middle of the night and managed to find a spot to sleep next to her, and yet a heaviness settled on her as she realized the serenity she had felt the day before had vanished.

She was too tired and discouraged to argue with the thoughts racing through her mind or fight with her feelings. *Sometimes I don't feel like I'm me.* She reached for her backpack and pulled out one of her notebooks, thumbing through it until she found what she was seeking: a poem she had written years ago.

I feel like I must have felt
when I was younger than five,
and he hurt me for the first time.
And I cut my hair and stared out the window,
the sunshine and laughter
gone from my life.
No feelings, no desires,
just emptiness.
But I adjusted, I changed,
I lost myself.

The sun, the bright-red, glowing sun,
hangs out there, so far away from view.
I feel like I'm in prison inside myself,
denying everything I am and want to be.
The sun is me,
alive, bright, glowing, giving life.
But I can't see it, I can't feel it
because I'm not me.

Closing her notebook, Dana quietly and defiantly whispered, "I'm not that person anymore. I *am* me!" She stood up and looked out the windows, disappointed to see dense fog. She pulled on fresh underwear and socks from her duffel and then slipped into the shirt and pants she had worn the day before. Grabbing a jacket, she climbed quietly down the spiral stairs, glancing in at Luke, who was sleeping soundly. Quickly she put on her boots by the door, signaled Sitka to stay, and slipped outside.

Walking around the house and down the stairs to the rocks, Dana could see only a few yards in front of her. She wondered briefly if she should change her mind and go back to the house. But she needed the solace of the water. She hungered to see it, touch it, smell it, hear it. And the thick, foggy air felt like a cocoon protecting her. She made her way to the spot where she'd noticed a pair of kayaks and a small canoe resting above the high tide line. She donned a life jacket and grabbed a canoe paddle, then placed the lightweight boat into the water. Carefully settling into the canoe, she began paddling through the calm water. As she circled the island, hugging the shore, the fog gradually cleared. A sea otter floated toward her, its head poking high above the water, watching her. She breathed deeply and forced herself to concentrate on the quietude around her, easing the turmoil and fatigue in her mind and body.

Dana paddled by the small cove strewn with clamshells where she had beachcombed the day before. As she drifted around the end of the island, retracing her route of a week ago, she caught her breath, marveling at the beauty before her. The volcano that dominated the mountain range in the distance was pink in the early-morning sun. A pair of seagulls flew low, skimming the flat surface of the bay. The distinctive call of a loon, haunting and unforgettable, reflected the magic of the moment.

Feeling refreshed and once again at peace, she paddled the canoe back toward her starting point. *The day can't possibly get any better than this,* she told herself.

As she approached the rocks below the stairs, she saw Luke stretched out on a flat rock nearby. Sitka was lying at the water's edge, close to where Dana had first seen him, and he woofed when he saw her.

"Good morning, you guys," Dana said, gliding to a stop.

Luke was immediately by her side. He stabilized the canoe as she got out and then hoisted it above his head.

"Thanks." Dana carefully skirted the slippery seaweed as she climbed the rocks. "I hope it was okay, my borrowing your canoe," she said. "I woke up early and couldn't sleep." She hugged Sitka, laughing as he tickled her face with his tongue.

"Sure," Luke said. "Anytime." He carried the canoe up the rocks and set it on the moss above the high tide line. He scanned the horizon. "Another nice day."

"It's beautiful!" Dana agreed, scratching Sitka's head.

She climbed up the stairs, with Luke and Sitka following close behind. Stopping at the railing of the large deck, which was cantilevered over a sheer drop-off, she looked toward the volcano. "I can't think of the words to describe the beauty here. It's more than the scenery—it's a *feeling*." Dana turned toward Luke. "The inspiration for your music comes from living here, doesn't it?"

"Partly. Though people and their lives also inspire me." Luke propelled Dana inside. "Right now I'm inspired to eat breakfast."

Dana laughed. "Me too."

For three days Luke showed Dana his world. They dip netted for red salmon in deep pools at the base of a waterfall. They fished for halibut and saw whales, porpoises, seals, sea lions, and countless sea otters. At high tide they caught pink salmon in a small lagoon, swatting no-see-ums between casts. At low tide they scoured the rocky tide pools and found anemones, chitons, snails, barnacles, tiny hermit crabs, and starfish, including the many-legged sunflower star.

When exploring the tide pools, Luke pried up a chiton and said, "You can eat these, you know. Friend of mine loves them. He was born in the Aleutians and eats them raw."

"Have you ever tried them?" Dana asked.

"Once. They were very chewy, kind of seemed like I was eating a piece of my belt, frankly. But the rocks are covered with them, so at least I won't starve if I get marooned over here for any length of time. The Dena'ina Indians used to steam them right on the rocks with boiling seaweed." He replaced the chiton, adding, "The variety they have in the West Indies must taste better—the local people there call them sea beef and consider them a delicacy." He then picked up a sea urchin and turned it over. "And did you know you can eat sea urchin eggs? You just scoop them out. They taste kinda sweet."

Wherever they went, Dana combed even the smallest exposed beach or tide pool for sea treasures. Soon almost every window ledge in Luke's home was covered with seashells, feathers, barnacle-covered rocks—anything that caught her eye.

While they were sailing the afternoon of the second day, Dana asked, "Have you fished your whole life?"

Luke shook his head. "Just since I came to Alaska. I was lucky. Sam, the fisherman I mentioned before, took a liking to me and taught me everything he knew. I sold my fishing boat and permit when Jamie got sick so I could spend all of my time with her. Now I occasionally work for a friend who's a builder, and I just fish for fun." Luke adjusted the trim of the sails as he prepared for a starboard tack.

Luke brought the bow around and pointed the boat into the wind, eased the main and jib sheets, and completed the turn. As he rounded out, he cleated off the sheets to the main and the jib, and the sails began to fill with wind.

Able to take his mind off the sails, he turned to Dana and asked, "What about you, Dana? I'll bet you were a straight-A student growing up."

"Well, Mom used to say she never had to worry about me. I was either daydreaming at our picture window or in my room reading. But I didn't stay inside all the time." Dana fingered the end of one of her braids. "My favorite times were the summers, when I'd go visit my grandparents. Their house is on a rocky bluff overlooking the ocean, and every morning I'd get up just before sunrise and walk to the tide pools. My room was on the ocean side, and the sound of the waves lulled me to sleep each night." She shrugged. "Pretty boring life."

Luke eyed her thoughtfully. "Somehow I get the feeling you're not telling me everything."

Luke's penetrating gaze made Dana uneasy, and she was silent for a full minute before responding. "Some things are difficult to talk about. I—Luke!" she gasped. "Look!" Dana pointed off the starboard bow. A small pod of black-and-white orcas was entering the mouth of the bay. "Killer whales!" Dana grabbed Luke's arm. "I've never seen them in the wild before!" she said excitedly. "Where's my camera?"

"Here it is," Luke said as he located Dana's Nikon and handed it to her.

"Thanks. Wow! Look at that!" The smaller whales chased one another and swam in circles. They leapt out of the water and slapped their tails at each other. "They're like a bunch of rambunctious kids playing."

"Well, that's just what they are. See that larger whale in the lead with the long, straight dorsal fin? That's an adult male. Male killer whales can have dorsal fins up to six feet long. The females and young orcas have smaller curved fins that look more like those of a dolphin."

"They're magnificent!" Dana clicked the shutter just as the large male raised his head out of the water like a giant periscope and slowly turned in a circle. "That should be a great photo!"

"That's called *spyhopping*. He's looking for jumping salmon—or maybe just checking us out."

"This is fantastic," Dana said exuberantly. "How often do you see them?"

"Fairly frequently when the salmon are running. This is a pod of resident coastal orcas, meaning they generally don't travel out of their home area. They feed on fish and are the most predictable and approachable of all the orcas. One time I looked up just as an orca breached about twenty feet into the air, spiraling its body. Talk about spectacular!"

"There they go!" Dana pointed as the whales disappeared from view behind a large peninsula. "Jeez, they're fast!"

Luke nodded. "They can swim up to thirty miles per hour."

Dana felt herself smiling broadly. "That's the best acrobatic show I've ever seen!" She leaned against the railing and sighed contentedly. "I could watch them for hours. I hope we see them again."

"Me too," Luke said. "I'm keeping a log of orca sightings for Alice's granddaughter. Part of a school project."

Dana looked at Luke appraisingly. "You're full of surprises."

Luke shrugged. "I enjoy it." The sails began to luff as the *Warm Breeze* started to lose the wind while passing a small island.

"So, can you recognize individual whales?" Dana asked.

"Sometimes. For instance, did you notice the gray patch behind their dorsal fins? It's called a saddle. No two are the same. Kind of like fingerprints. And each dorsal fin is also different, though the fins change as the whales grow.

"There are also transient coastal orcas," Luke continued, "which travel in smaller groups than the pod we just saw. These orcas don't have fixed territories, and they feed on seals, sea lions, porpoises, and occasionally even sea birds. They can be seen in this area as well, but they don't interact with the resident pods. Oh, and there are also offshore orcas. Not much is known about them, although they eat marine mammals, fish, and squid."

"How did you learn so much about whales?" Dana asked.

"Well..." Luke paused as he eased the mainsail to collect the light air. "While the *Warm Breeze* was being built, Jamie and I frequently stayed with friends who lived near the boatyard. We saw lots of killer whales—Jamie especially because she wasn't feeling well and would often sit on our friends' front porch and look out across the water. It reminded her of being on the island." He briefly gazed toward the distant horizon. "It's funny, I can talk about Jamie a little easier now. I guess maybe I hadn't put it all behind me as well as I thought I had."

Dana touched his hand, and squeezed it. He squeezed hers back.

"At any rate, when the sunset was particularly colorful, we noticed the whales seemed to enjoy it too. At least, they became very playful and active at sunset. Other times, especially on foggy days, we'd see them resting close together. And sometimes they'd be traveling side by side in a line."

"Like Neptune's synchronized swimmers."

"Exactly. I read somewhere each pod of whales has its own

distinctive dialect. Captive whales have even been traced back to their original pods."

"Amazing," Dana said.

Luke smiled. "Yeah. And orcas are pretty attached to their moms, even as they get older. Apparently they're a matriarchal society. Moms and their young are easy to identify, but not so with dads. Even the large males follow their mothers all of their lives."

"Just like with some humans, some animals are more attached to their mothers than anyone else," Dana mused.

Luke looked at her quizzically, but she zipped up her jacket and pretended not to notice his expression. "Have you heard of Moby Doll?"

"Yep," Luke answered without hesitation. "One of the first orcas—and actually a male—held in captivity. And that was in the mid-sixties, at the aquarium in Vancouver, BC."

"Don't look so smug," she retorted. "I'm sure I'll think of a question you won't be able to answer."

Luke's tender gaze held Dana's a long moment. "Until then you can't leave," he joshed, and she smiled.

Chapter Eight

After breakfast on the fourth morning, Luke left Dana and Sitka searching through the tide pools in front of the house while he motored in the inflatable Zodiac out to the *Warm Breeze* to collect a couple of clam rakes. On his return, he tied up the small boat in the cove and had just set out on the trail to the house when he became aware of piano music in the still morning air. Surprised, Luke stopped briefly and listened, entranced.

He continued on his way, walking up the stairs and crossing the deck as quietly as possible, not wanting to disturb Dana. He paused again when he caught sight of her through the window, telling himself he would always remember that moment: Dana's beautiful face tranquil and unguarded as she poured her heart into a tune he didn't recognize. It was clear that whatever emotions she kept to herself she expressed through her music, just as he did.

Sensing Luke's presence, Dana abruptly stopped playing.

"Don't stop," Luke pleaded as he entered the room. "You play beautifully."

"I don't usually play in front of anyone." Dana said, blushing. "When I was growing up, I played a lot of ragtime, like 'Twelfth Street Rag.' I put thumbtacks on the hammers of my piano to give it a honky-tonk sound."

"May I join you?"

"Okay," Dana said shyly and slid over on the piano bench.

Luke sat down to Dana's right. "The guitar isn't the only instrument I play, you know," Luke said. "I've got a few classics up my sleeve." He flexed his fingers, carefully placed them on the ivory keys, and proceeded to play "Chopsticks."

Dana burst out laughing and played the accompaniment. "Do you know 'Heart and Soul'?"

Luke replied by launching into the melody. They played several other simple duets before exhausting Luke's repertoire.

"Bravo!" Dana clapped.

"Sometimes I even surprise myself."

Still laughing, Dana admitted, "I've had more fun with you these last few days than I've had in as long as I can remember, maybe forever."

Luke suspected she hadn't had much fun as a little girl. He said, "I saw a button once that said, *It's never too late to have a happy childhood.*"

Dana smiled. "I do like *that* idea."

Gently taking her hand, Luke said, "Good. Let's go clamming."

As usual, Sitka took the lead, and the threesome walked along the trail to the cove. Minutes later they set off in the Zodiac to a nearby beach. Sitka jumped out and disappeared into the grassy area above the tide line, almost completely hidden except for his bushy tail waving like a flag.

Luke secured the boat while Dana unloaded a five-gallon plastic bucket and the clam rakes. She remarked how amazed she was at the difference between the extreme high and low tides. "Yeah," Luke replied, "with today's low tide of almost minus five feet, the difference is about twenty-eight feet of tidal range."

"Wow! That really changes the landscape."

"It sure does." Luke took one of the rakes and pointed to a stream of water squirting from the rocky beach. "Okay, Dana, here's what you do. First you look for a squirt like that one, and then you dig through the rocks like this." He began raking and exposed several butter clams. "The trick is to look for the clams near the mussel line. That's where you find them."

Dana took the other clam rake and followed Luke's instructions, uncovering a bed of clams. "I didn't think it would be this easy," she commented as she picked out the clams. "I'm used to digging razor clams in the sand, where they burrow away from you as fast as you try to grab them."

"We have razor clams too, on the inlet beaches north of here. But I like the taste of these better. And they're much easier to clean."

Soon they had a large pile of succulent butter clams that they tossed into the bucket. Luke deemed the quantity sufficient, adding, "We'll put some cornmeal and fresh seawater in with the clams when we get back. The clams filter the cornmeal out of the water they take in, which helps to clean them."

He whistled for Sitka to hop into the Zodiac and then turned to Dana. "What do you say we steam these in beer for dinner and dip them in butter? Almost as delicious as shrimp. We need to save some for chowder, though. You haven't lived until you've tried some of my chowder."

"And I assume you know where the word *chowder* comes from?" Dana asked with a grin.

Luke laughed. "Of course. The story goes that some shipwrecked sailors stranded on the Maine coast a couple of hundred years ago threw all the food they could salvage from the ship, along with clams from the beach, into a big pot called a *chaudiere.* And voilà! New England clam chowder was born."

After dinner, Luke carried a stack of wood up the stairs to the deck. Dana was watering the flowers, humming as she worked.

Luke paused and studied her, thinking how lovely she was. Her loosened hair was remarkable—thick, curly, and a rich auburn—and her luminous dark-brown eyes sat above a few freckles sprinkled across her face. She seemed totally and refreshingly unaware of her arresting beauty and radiated an innocent goodness that left Luke in awe. She was genuine, honest, and sincere. And full of surprises.

For probably the hundredth time, he wondered what was troubling her and wished he could help. He considered the times he'd seen her sitting on the rocks, Sitka by her side, her notebook in her lap. She would stare across the water with her knees drawn up to her chin, looking lonely and lost. Then suddenly she would pick up her notebook and fill page after page.

The day before, Luke had finally broached the subject by asking lightly, "Do I have the honor of knowing a future best-selling author?"

The haunted look in her eyes was hidden behind her quick smile. Nevertheless she had admitted, "I write so I won't be alone."

Knowing how private Dana was, Luke felt almost ecstatic she had chosen to share that small intimacy with him. But he also realized his elation was a function of his increasing attraction to her, and he wasn't sure how to handle that. Sometimes it took all of his willpower not to take her in his arms and kiss her. But he was happy she was there with him, and he would never compromise her trust.

Dana refilled the watering can to water the plants on the small deck outside her tower room. She climbed the spiral staircase and then stepped out onto the deck, enjoying the panoramic view from her tree-top height. After watering the flowers, she sat on the bench to admire the vibrant, lush blooms. She wished she could have been on the island when Luke and Jake were planting the flowers. There was something satisfying and soothing about digging holes in moist soil, mounding the soil around a delicate stem, and by so doing, giving life to a colorful blossom.

The sound of an ax splitting wood caught her attention, and she looked over the railing. Luke, naked to the waist, stood whacking a maul cleanly through log rounds, his movements fluid and rhythmic. Unexpectedly, and to her great surprise, Dana's pulse raced. She wanted to run her hands along his lean, muscular body; she wanted to feel his naked skin next to hers. *What's going on here?* she asked herself, shocked at her reaction to him. Sexual desire overwhelmed her and jolted every nerve like a live wire.

Almost reeling from the realization of her intense attraction to Luke, Dana decided she needed a calming soak in the hot tub before coming face-to-face with him again. She changed into the T-shirt and Mickey Mouse shorts that doubled as her bathing suit and slipped down the stairs to the deck. As she sank into the hot tub, at its perfect ninety-nine degrees, Dana pushed aside all thoughts of her unexpected physical longing for Luke.

Sighing with pleasure, she leaned back and let her arms float to the surface. She was more relaxed than she'd been in weeks, maybe years, maybe forever. She closed her eyes and felt her worries dissipate in the soothing warmth.

"Ah, there you are."

Dana's eyes flew open. Luke was smiling down at her. "I think I might have dozed off," she said. "Are you done splitting wood?"

"Yeah. Just finished. I thought I'd play for you if you're up for another serenade." He hefted the guitar as he sat on the bench.

Dana nodded. "Always. How long have you been playing, anyway?"

"Since I was about twelve. My best friend showed me the basics, and I taught myself the rest."

"Your music is so expressive. It's as if I can hear your thoughts and your emotions when you play."

He smiled and strummed a few bars. "I guess that means I accomplish what I hope to." He played a bit more. "If in telling my story it touches people in some way, well…" Luke shrugged and continued playing.

Dana leaned her head against the edge of the hot tub and once again closed her eyes, listening to Luke weaving his magic. The soft, melodious sounds relaxed her, comforted her, healed her. She floated into another reality, free from her past torment. Like his island, Luke's music provided a refuge that enveloped her. Her mind drifted without restraint, unencumbered by the past.

When she finally reopened her eyes, the sun was beginning to set—promising another gorgeous sunset that would change colors several times before it darkened into the gradually lengthening night of the waning Alaska summer. Dana watched Luke play his guitar, eyes closed, completely caught up in the music.

She hadn't planned on telling him about her childhood. The subject was too personal, too revealing, too horrible. But in that moment she realized her lifelong fears had melted away, and she wasn't afraid anymore. She wanted to tell him, to unburden herself of the secret she'd been carrying for most of her life.

"Luke, I'd like to—" She paused and stepped out of the hot tub, wrapping herself snugly in a thick towel. Then she walked to the edge of the deck, wringing her hands. *This isn't going to be as easy as I thought.*

Maybe she should just give up trying to figure things out, go home, and marry Mark. They were used to each other and comfortable together. Maybe that was enough.

Dana paced back and forth along the wide deck, staring across the bay.

Or maybe there was a reason she was on this island with Luke. Maybe it was easier to confide in someone you'd never see again.

Finally she walked over and sat down facing Luke, who had set aside his guitar but otherwise had not moved and was watching her intently. She took a deep breath and said, "I want to tell you about my past."

"Are you sure?" Luke asked carefully.

She nodded. "I have to figure out how to...let go. I don't want this to haunt me for the rest of my life."

Dana sat very still, gathering her thoughts. Her face was emotionless. Then quietly, almost in a whisper, she began, looking out at the bay as she spoke.

"My dad died in a car accident when I was very young. My mom was in the accident too, but miraculously she was uninjured. She died a couple of years ago. Anyway, my dad's brother moved into our house to help my mother cope."

Dana unconsciously twisted her hair as she spoke. "It wasn't long before my uncle...my uncle started raping me. I had a strong will and resisted as much as I could. But each time I refused, he would do something worse to me."

"My God, Dana." Luke's voice was tight. "How old were you?"

"The abuse started when I was about four and ended when I was eight." Dana sighed weakly, relieved she had told him that part. The rest...well, suddenly she knew she would keep the rest to herself.

"Even though I accept that it happened, and obviously I can't change the fact that it did, recently I realized that not being able to let go of the past has bogged me down in a mire of needing to feel bad, be unhappy, and punish myself. I'm comfortable in my misery, and that scares me. I need to break the pattern, if that's what it is. I know I have to let the bad feelings flow out of me. I just don't know how." A single tear rolled down her cheek.

She looked at Luke. "Your hurt over losing your wife—you've been able to let go of the past and pull yourself together, and I admire that. That's what I want to do too. Let go of the past once and for all. I mean, I know they're completely different circumstances. One was a natural event, the other—well, it was completely unnatural. But we both suffered terrible pain as a result." She stopped speaking. Clouds now covered the darkening sky. The only sound was the incoming tide lapping against the rocks.

Luke finally broke the silence. In a voice filled with rage, he said, "He was a monster."

Dana put her hand on his arm. "Luke, your anger helps me. I was never angry as a child; I just kept asking myself why. I'm more able to feel my anger at this point. Therapy has helped with that. What's important to me now is…" She looked away from him, unsure of how to continue. "My past has affected my relationship with Mark. I'm not very experienced when it comes to making love—Mark is my first and only—and I'm always holding back. Sometimes when we're…when Mark and I are…my uncle's face is all I can see, and his voice is all I can hear. Making love confuses me. The images with the…certain images are appearing more and more frequently, and I'm afraid of what's happening. I feel like I'm sliding backward, not moving forward. Lately I'm more uncomfortable with sex than I've ever been."

Dana rose abruptly and walked to the edge of the deck, staring into the inky water. A stiff breeze swirled tendrils of auburn hair around her face. She turned to face Luke, who was looking at her with such compassion and sadness it made her heart ache, and said in a barely audible voice, "I need to know love doesn't have to hurt."

Dana excused herself shortly after that, assuring Luke she was all right, just feeling a little drained. "Think I'll call it a night."

Luke nodded. "Let me know if you need anything."

"Thanks," Dana said quietly and stepped inside the house.

Luke could not get over what Dana's uncle had done. It was horrifying, a news story on a channel he would change if he could because he couldn't bear the gross injustice—a vulnerable little child confronted by an adult who abdicates his role as her protector and betrays her wide-eyed trust. But Luke couldn't change this channel. This had happened to someone he lov—to someone he knew. And cared deeply about.

He knew his response had been inadequate, but he also knew that nothing he could ever say or ever do would fix the past, and he felt like everything he said or did now would muddle the present. How do you put into words the anguish you feel for another person? The helplessness? The anger? How do you say, "Let me help," and really mean it, when you don't know what to do?

Chapter Nine

Dana got up early the next day and walked with Sitka to the rock bridge, picking blueberries along the trail. The fruit was plump and ripe, hanging heavily on the branches. Dana picked the berries carefully, selecting only the perfect ones. Luke had explained that any distortion in the berry surface generally meant an insect larva dwelt inside. He further explained that all you had to do was soak them in water and the worms crawled out. She, however, preferred searching for wormless berries.

Dana and Sitka crossed the rock bridge to the point, one of Dana's favorite spots on Luke's island. She sat down in the moss, leaning back against the same fallen log she and Luke had leaned against the day she arrived. Sitka lay beside her, nuzzling her hand to be petted. Dana happily obliged.

"Mark would really like it here, Sitka. He loves the water as much as I do." She sat cross-legged, her right hand continuously stroking her steadfast friend.

A symphony of gentle sounds surrounded her. The water lapped against the rocks that rose steeply on this end of the island. Birds trilled. A gentle breeze whispered through the boughs of the trees.

She'd been here almost a week now, and the trappings of everyday life had melted away. She was in another world, without phones and with minimal electricity, generated by wind and sun. Living by the sunrise and sunset, by the ebb and flow of the tides, and by the vagaries of the weather, Dana existed in a block of time and space untouched by other humans, unfettered by their problems, their joys, or their politics. Though removed from her everyday life, she still had all the comforts of home.

Dana rummaged in her backpack for her notebook—another new one!—and found a note from Mark inserted behind the cover.

> *I've been trying to keep my notes to you short and sweet, and I've been trying not to intrude on your time away. But there are a few things I need to say.*
>
> *I still remember so clearly how, as kids, I'd find you crying and even though I asked, you wouldn't tell me why. You'd just wipe away your tears and ask if my mom was going to have pizza for dinner that night and could you have dinner with us. Melted cheese makes everything better, you always said, and still do.*

Dana smiled and continued reading.

> *I didn't understand what had happened to you as a child until you told me when we were adults. I was horrified and shocked and also amazed that you seemed to be so "to- gether" in spite of the terrible things that happened to you. I am ashamed to say I was grateful for that. Sometimes I think I had better instincts as a young kid than I do as an adult. And I confess I don't adequately relate to your pain, even now. Maybe because my childhood was so ordinary and problem-free.*
>
> *I know we've had our problems for a while, and what happened with my copilot that one time didn't help...*

Dana put Mark's note back in her notebook without finishing it. She loved Mark and had forgiven him. She had moved on. She needed to focus on herself and the healing process she felt had finally begun.

Taking a deep breath, Dana inhaled the scent of the damp moss and the decaying logs and the saltwater. She was lost in her thoughts as she rubbed Sitka's ears. *I know I'm making progress,* she told herself. *I know I am. I can't accept being somewhere in between anymore, or at a comfort level that only keeps me from going over the edge but not moving forward. I have to keep pushing myself to the limit to get to where I want to be: serene, happy, at peace.*

After so many years of not feeling, I'm going to allow myself to feel—without torment or conflict.

I won't let my uncle win. I have to figure out a way to break his hold on me. I just can't think of how to do it. Maybe I'm thinking too much. Maybe I need to feel my way through it, again and again, until there's nothing more to feel. But when will the bad feelings stop coming with the good?

Say yes to myself. Be in control. Don't be afraid. He can't hurt me anymore. Let the feelings go. Let them flow through me and out of me, swept away by the outgoing tide, washed away by the cleansing rain, borne off by the ocean breezes.

Sitka sat up, and Dana became aware of Luke approaching on the moss and coming to a stop behind her. His presence was comforting rather than intrusive, and it swathed her in warmth.

"It's so easy to feel safe here," she said, turning to him.

Luke smiled. "I'm glad." He sat down beside her, lightly touching her arm. "Dana, does Mark know about your uncle?"

She nodded. "Yes. When I told him, he finally understood what had been troubling me when we were kids. Eventually what had happened to me started causing problems between us, especially after my mom died a couple of years ago. I think the emotional stress of losing her contributed to my inability to deal with my childhood memories and feelings. When Mark wanted to make love and I didn't, I couldn't say no. I allowed him to make love to me when I didn't want to, and that only reinforced what I learned as a child: that love hurts. And now we're in this behavior pattern that is detrimental to our relationship and that I'm desperately fighting to overcome."

Dana took a deep breath, fingering the moss on the log, wanting Luke to understand. "Because I grew up thinking love was supposed to hurt, I made sure it did. Subconsciously I tried to re-create what I learned about love from my childhood experience. I need to stop feeling sad, burdened, and hurt through love. I need to feel *I'm* the one in control, not my uncle. I need to take back my life; I just don't know how."

Dana nuzzled Sitka's face before continuing. "My uncle did some things to me I've never been able to tell anyone, not even Mark. Maybe if I *had* told him…" Dana hesitated, unable to look at Luke. Instead she stared at the bay in front of them.

When she spoke again, her voice was constricted. She was talking more to herself than to Luke. "Maybe my life would be easier if I were with someone new instead of trying to work out my problems with Mark. But I love him, and we share so much history, which is one of the things that keeps us together. It also causes a wedge between us, at least from my point of view.

"Mark's been willing to put up with my sexual problems. He tries to understand why I'm the way I am and hopes I'll be different someday. If not, he says it doesn't matter, that he'll still be with me. He just prays I'll get things figured out. He loves me more than anything else in the world and wants to marry me."

Dana looked across the water and asked, "But how can I marry him when passion and desire are missing? I hope those emotions are somewhere inside me, waiting for me to figure out how to access them and join that part of myself with the rest of me so I can love—in my heart and with my body—completely and without reservation."

As Dana talked, Luke's conflicted feelings threatened to overwhelm him. He wanted to comfort Dana, hold her tenderly, but feared that would be the worst thing for her. Plus, he had no idea what to think of her disclosures about her relationship with Mark. How could he help her when he was at a complete loss as to what to say or do? Or when he wanted to make love to her so badly he actually ached from desire?

Not knowing what to say, he took her berry-stained hands in his own. "I see you've been picking blueberries."

"Yep. I was hoping to talk you into fixing some of your famous pancakes."

"You're on! Glad to hear you have an appetite."

Walking back to the house, they fell into light and easy conversation, avoiding anything remotely related to her revelations of a few minutes before. They lingered over breakfast, each enjoying a second helping of pancakes.

"Dana..." Luke hesitated, unsure what to say. "Having you here has been great."

Dana smiled warmly. "It's been wonderful for me too." She stood up and said, "It's a beautiful day. Let's finish our coffee outside."

"Sounds good to me," Luke replied.

They relaxed on the small raised deck partially surrounding the hot tub, enjoying the quiet sounds of the early morning: a pair of bald eagles was audible in the distance, calling to each other; a red squirrel ran up a nearby tree, chattering excitedly; the incoming tide lapped at the rocks.

Dana surprised Luke when she asked, "May I stay a little longer?"

Luke worked to keep the elation out of his voice. "Of course. You're welcome to stay as long as you like."

"Thanks. Being here is helping me to sort things out."

"I'm glad." Luke gazed over the water and then back at Dana. Could she possibly be staying because of him? He tried to read her feelings in her eyes. Despite his struggle with his enormous attraction to her, he realized he wanted her to stay no matter what the reason.

Lightly Dana touched Luke's arm. "I need to let Mark know how to get in touch with me in case of an emergency."

"Oh. Sure." Was his disappointment obvious? He hoped not. "I'm due for a food run. You can call him from town."

"Actually…I'm not ready to go back to the real world." Dana picked at Sitka's underfur. "I was thinking of writing him a letter instead—if you wouldn't mind mailing it for me."

"Sure thing. I need to stop by the post office and pick up my junk mail anyway."

"How should I tell him to contact me if he needs to?" she asked.

"You've heard the local bushline on the public radio station, right?"

Dana nodded. "Just after the news."

"I'll give you their number. All Mark has to do is call them and ask them to send you a bushline. They broadcast each message three times a day for two days. Simple as that. Tell him you'll listen to the radio at least once a day, just in case."

"Great. That's easy enough." She got up and stretched. "I think I'll go to the cove and soak up the sun while I write the letter." She smiled sheepishly. "Oh, and do you have a spare envelope?"

Luke scribbled the station's phone number on a scrap of paper and handed it to Dana. He then rummaged in a drawer and came out with a small envelope. "How about if I meet you in the cove in, say, an hour?" he asked.

She saluted with the envelope. "Perfect."

Finding a relatively flat area on the rocks overlooking the cove, Dana sat down and for a while just enjoyed the warmth of the morning sunshine and the sights and sounds around her. The incoming tide sounded like a rushing stream as it flowed through the narrow channel separating that end of the island from the verdant mountain slope on the opposite side. Wisps of white clouds moved languorously across the sky, gradually changing shape. A bird trilled from high in a nearby tree. The howl of a coyote, followed by an answering call, floated over the water from the mainland.

Wilderness filled every vantage point. Luke's island was located within an undeveloped state park, one of the few inholdings, and he was the only year-round resident in the area. Only a few vacation cabins dotted the large fjord, all at least several miles from Luke's home and none visible. Dana found the feeling of isolation welcome and complete.

She took her notebook and pen from her backpack and set to the task at hand.

Dear Mark,
I've found a place—a small, remote island—where I feel safe.
It's tranquil and comforting, and the beauty is indescribable.
The first night I was here I watched swirls of foam rise
and fall over some rocks with the incoming tide. I remember

feeling real panic for the rocks, thinking, You'll suffocate! But I guess I was just seeing myself in times past, living in an abyss of no hope, unable to do anything, waiting for time to swallow me up.

You know how often I've been bogged down by painful memories, unable to find my way through them. But here my thoughts and feelings have been tumbling and rushing out, like a dam that's been broken. I've been doing a lot of writing, and you know how much that helps me.

Sometimes I still feel like I'm two people, and we're waging a war. The person who I truly am is inside me, trying to get out, but the someone else won't let me. She's still stronger than the real me.

I hate it when she's in control. She doesn't let me feel anything except hurt. She doesn't know anything about love or making love except that it hurts. It's a battle between feeling good about love and sex and feeling scared. Maybe that doesn't sound like I'm making progress, but I know I am. I'm beginning to put things in their proper perspective, and I'm trying to let go of the past.

You've always been there for me, always, despite our problems. I know how much you love me and how special you think I am. I'm beginning to believe I might finally be able to return your love, the way I know I should—the way I want to and the way you deserve.

I'm not sure how much longer I'll be here. I know how hard my indecisiveness is for you, and I'm being unfair to ask you to keep waiting. But I finally feel like I'm starting to sort things out, and I know things will be better for us in the end. Much better.

Dana closed her letter with the information on how Mark could reach her in an emergency and sent him her love. She had just sealed her letter when Luke strode up to the Zodiac, Sitka at his heels, and began untying the inflatable boat.

Dana hurriedly scrawled the address on the envelope and scrambled down the rocks. "Perfect timing," she told Luke. "I'm all done."

Luke pocketed Dana's letter. "I'll mail it as soon as I get to town so I don't forget. Sitka, do you want to come with me or stay here with Dana?"

In reply, Sitka sat down beside Dana, who steadied the Zodiac as Luke climbed in.

Luke grinned. "I should have known." He started the outboard. "I'm beginning to wonder whose dog he is!"

"Well, I'm glad for the company," Dana said, petting Sitka's head.

"I'll be back before dinner."

"Take your time. I'm not going anywhere!" Dana shoved the Zodiac off the rocks and waved as Luke headed for the *Warm Breeze* through the glassy water.

Chapter Ten

LUKE WAS PREOCCUPIED WITH THOUGHTS OF DANA THE ENTIRE time he was running his errands. He thought about the increasing physical contact they'd had, the occasional touch, a helping hand lingering longer each time, the warm hug Dana had given him when he left for town that morning—in fact, she had seemed reluctant to let go of him. He thought about the shy, thoughtful look in her eyes when she glanced at him and didn't think he saw her. He thought about how happy she was on the island, how at ease they felt with each other, how well they got along...

Could she possibly be as attracted to him as he was to her? On one hand, she sure seemed to be in no hurry to go home, and he certainly didn't think he was imagining the chemistry between them. But on the other hand, did she think of him as just a really good friend—someone with whom she had a great deal in common and someone to confide in because she felt a kinship with him she didn't feel with Mark? Though if that were the case, why would she be considering marrying the guy?

Luke, you're just gonna drive yourself crazy if you keep this up, he told himself.

He decided to stop by the Mariner to check in with Jake before heading home and strolled up the beach to his favorite haunt. Once inside, he made a beeline for the bar, where his old friend was holding court, as usual. Always on stage, Jake loved to mingle with the patrons, entertaining them with his stories.

Often he would demonstrate his flamboyant drink-mixing style. A favorite local pastime was suggesting an obscure concoction in an attempt to stump Jake. But his repertoire was vast, and so far no one had bested him.

Jake had befriended Luke the day Luke arrived in town. They took to each other immediately, and Jake soon considered Luke the son he never had. Jake knew everyone in town, especially the fishermen. Knowing Luke was looking for work, he had introduced him to Sam, who ran several boats and often needed help. It was an introduction that had changed Luke's life.

Luke grinned as he approached the bar. Jake was so engrossed in telling his latest tale he didn't notice his protégé. "Don't believe a word he says," Luke good-humoredly told the customers, interrupting Jake's commentary.

"Luke, my boy!" Jake came around the bar and gave Luke a bear hug. "Good to see you. Listen, hang on just a second." He went back and served the drink he was preparing with a flourish, declaring, "And that's my version of a silver cloud. Now, excuse me, folks. I need to visit with my long-lost son. Rosie, take over!" he called to his assistant. "I'll be outside with Luke."

Rosie nodded. "Glad he finally turned up."

Jake and Luke ambled out onto the deck that overlooked the bay and leaned on the railing. They had the deck to themselves. This time of day was the lull between lunch and dinner, before most patrons arrived to relax after a day of fishing, hiking, or shopping.

"You've been a mite scarce around here lately," Jake said in a voice half admonishing and half curious.

Luke self-consciously adjusted his baseball cap. "Yeah, guess I have."

"So...where is she?" Jake asked, glancing around the deck. "Who?"

Jake snorted. "Who. Dana, of course!"

"She's on the island with Sitka."

"*With Sitka?!*" Jake hooted and slapped Luke on the back. "I was right. This *is* serious, for you to leave Sitka with her."

"What are you talking about?" Luke asked, defensive.

"You and Dana." Jake spoke as if anyone would have drawn the same conclusion. "Many's the lass who wiped away a tear when I broke the news you were taken."

"You did what?"

"Well, obviously, from the way you talked about Dana a couple of weeks ago, I assumed as much. Besides, I haven't seen you since then. You don't often pass up a chance to play at locals' night."

Luke shrugged. "I've been showing Dana the sights."

"The sights, eh?" Jake winked and laughed.

"Jake, you've got it all wrong. She came to Alaska to work some things out. Like, if she wants to marry Mark, her boyfriend, for one. I just offered to let her sort through her problems on the island."

"And by the by, you fell for her." Jake's voice was gentle. "Hard."

Damn but Jake was perceptive. Luke removed his baseball cap and scratched his forehead. He tried to explain what he had only begun to understand himself. "When I'm around her, I want to tell her what I'm thinking and how I'm feeling. I also feel protective of her and want to take care of her." Luke sighed. "This is the first time since Jamie died I've met someone I want to get to know."

"I know how much you loved Jamie and how devoted you were to her," Jake said. "I also know she'd want you to get on with your life."

Luke shook his head. "I can't ask Dana to stay with me."

"Why not?" Jake looked at Luke with frustration. "You've fallen in love with her, haven't you?"

Luke was startled at the question. He was even more startled when he answered without hesitation, "Yes."

"Does she feel the same way about you?"

Luke shrugged. "She doesn't want to leave yet, I do know that."

"So, what's the problem?"

"Like I said, she's practically engaged. That's a problem, don't you think?"

"Is she aware of your feelings for her?"

Luke hesitated for a few seconds. "I honestly don't know."

"Have you told her?"

"I haven't wanted to influence her."

"Look, okay, she has some problems she's trying to work out." Jake threw up his hands in apparent exasperation. "I can understand you don't want to be another complication in her life. But wouldn't she have married this guy if she really loved him?"

"Life's not that simple."

"Life never is." Jake stroked his long beard. "One thing's for sure. You're head over heels. And I don't want to see you hurt again."

"I appreciate your concern, Jake. I don't know what will happen. She seems both determined and reluctant to return to her boyfriend. Maybe I'm only here to help her and provide a haven where she can let go of what's troubling her. Maybe she loves the island and Sitka, not me."

"If you feel better thinking like that, go ahead," Jake grumbled. "But it's entirely possible Dana might have to go home to whatever his name is before she realizes who she really loves."

"As hard as it is, I will not ask her to stay," Luke replied. "When she leaves, if she says she's going home to be with Mark,

I'll have to believe her and go on with my life. Maybe she'll come back; maybe she won't."

It was late afternoon by the time Luke returned. He anchored the sailboat and was gathering the groceries he had stowed in the galley for the trip across the bay when he noticed the coffee tin with Jamie's handwritten note attached. Jake had told him a couple of their friends had started roasting and selling coffee beans, and Luke had stopped by to see them, purchasing a new blend they had just roasted. Luke had realized, especially after his talk with Jake, that it was time for a change—no matter where Dana's heart lay. After he poured the new blend into the tin, he grabbed one corner of Jamie's note and ripped it off quickly, like a Band-Aid.

With a deep sigh and glad he'd made that symbolic gesture, Luke climbed into the Zodiac and motored to the cove. Once he'd tied up, he started down the trail, wondering if Dana might have seen him arrive and be walking toward the cove to meet him. He realized he had only been apart from her for a few hours, yet he had missed her almost to distraction. Could she possibly be having the same feelings about him?

The connection they had immediately forged had quickly strengthened and developed into a deep and trusting friendship. She was obviously happy and comfortable with him and able to relax and have fun—something that, from what she had said, she hadn't been able to do for a long time. He made her laugh. A lot. But maybe being with him felt *too* good. Made her feel disloyal to Mark.

And just as it was obvious she enjoyed Luke's company, it was equally obvious she loved Mark. She'd loved him her whole life. Her plan had been to come here, work out her problems, and go home and marry him.

"Dammit, what should I do?" he asked aloud, his words carried away by the breeze. "Should I tell her how I feel or keep it to myself? The last thing I want to do is upset her."

He impatiently shook his head. He wouldn't find the answer to his dilemma by dwelling on it—that was certain.

As he approached the boardwalk, he spotted Dana and Sitka stretched out in the sun on the rock ledge in front of the house. Dana was apparently asleep and didn't hear his return. Sitka, though, was already bounding up the stairs to greet him. That woke Dana up, and he called down to her from the deck. She looked up at him, smiling brightly, and waved. Luke felt his heart do a backflip.

He caught Dana up on his trip to town, leaving out his conversation about her with Jake. But a short while later as they prepared dinner, Luke thought about Jake's question. How *did* Dana feel about him? Her initial shyness had fast disappeared, and she seemed very much at ease with him, often laughing and joking. They shared a love of music, nature, the sea, animals, books. He felt certain she was attracted to him, but was she even aware of it? Would she allow herself to be aware of it? What *was* she feeling? How much *could* she feel in light of everything that had happened to her? Well, she would be staying at least a little while longer, it seemed. At this point, he couldn't ask for anything more. Hell, he couldn't ask for *anything*—or wouldn't—no matter how much he wanted to. He would be there for Dana and see her through, no matter what happened.

Who am I kidding? Luke asked himself, interrupting his righteous reflections. *I love her, and I don't want her to leave. Ever.*

After dinner, Luke pulled a small bag from his pocket. "I have something for you. Picked it up in town today." He handed the bag to Dana.

She opened it carefully and peered inside. "Oh, Luke, it's beautiful!" she exclaimed and threw her arms around his neck. "Thank you so much." She upended the contents into her hand and closely studied the small pale-pink shell.

Luke smiled at her obvious delight. "It's called a precious wentletrap. Name comes from the Dutch word for a winding staircase."

"It's beautiful. And absolutely perfect." She cocked her head. "I've looked in most of the shops in town, but I never saw this shell."

"I got it from Jake. He has his own collection."

"He does?" she asked in wonderment. "Gosh, the more I know about him, the more I like him."

Luke grinned. "That's what all the women say." He nodded at the shell. "He said that in the seventeen and eighteen hundreds, these shells were quite rare; in fact, replicas were made from rice paste and sold for a pretty high price."

"Wow! How interesting! " Dana smiled at Luke. "Thank you again. Every time I look at it, I'll think of your wonderful spiral staircase." She rubbed her finger over the shell's surface. "I've loved shells since I was a little girl. How did you know I collected them?"

Luke chuckled. "Well, the fact you've got almost all the window ledges in the house covered with shells you've found gave me a pretty good clue."

Dana's expression sobered, and she turned the shell over and over in her hand. "You have no idea how much this means to me."

Luke saw the flash of pain in her eyes. He stayed silent, expecting a new revelation. He didn't have to wait long.

"When I was young and visited my grandparents, I used to comb the beaches for the most perfect shells I could find," Dana said. "To me they represented hope. If all those delicate shells could remain intact despite the violence of the wind and waves, their hostile environment, maybe survival was possible—maybe *anything* was possible.

"I remember one day in particular when I found a triton shell in perfect condition." Dana's face softened at the memory. "I carefully held it in my hand and imagined the refuge it had once provided. It gave me the strength to go on."

Clutching the wentletrap shell to her heart, Dana slowly crossed the space that separated her and Luke. She took his hand and gazed into his eyes. "Being here with you is also helping me believe anything is possible."

Luke's senses came alive with her touch, and a jumble of emotions washed over him. Dana certainly seemed to be conveying how she felt about him, and he wanted nothing more than to take her in his arms and make love to her. But he didn't want to confuse matters for her—even though it was she who seemed to be reaching out. Reluctantly he pulled his eyes from hers and looked outside. The water was like glass. "Perfect night for kayaking," he managed to say. "Would you like to go?"

Dana stepped to the window. "Yes, I'd love to."

The moment was broken, and they were back to being just friends. Luke was both relieved and disappointed.

They slid the kayaks into the calm water and started paddling around the island. Sitka followed them as long as he could by running along the rocks. Eventually the rocks became too steep and Sitka ran back toward the house, no doubt to wait at his favorite spot, the small grassy area from which the distant volcano dominated the horizon.

"This is perfect," Dana said, pleasure obvious in her voice, as they passed a gravel spit jutting from the farthest end of the island. "Kayaking lets you feel like you're part of the water, connected to it somehow, don't you think? It's almost as if the serenity of the water seeps through the skin of the boat and into your body."

"I couldn't have put it better myself," Luke agreed. He was still trying to get his feelings for Dana under control, and whenever she said something like this that reached in and touched him deeply, his longing for her only increased.

Circumnavigating the island, they passed the *Warm Breeze* and were approaching the cove when Luke pointed out a tall spruce tree among the others. "See that large, dark area halfway up that tree?"

"I think so," Dana said, squinting. "Yes. Yes, I do."

"That's the eagles' nest, the one we walked to the other day."

"And every year they return?"

"So far."

"This would be a wonderful place to raise kids," she said, seemingly more to herself than to Luke.

"Do you want to have any, Dana?" he asked.

"Someday. That's why Mark would like to get married soon. He's wanted to have children for a long time. One of the reasons I've been putting him off is because figuring out my own problems takes up enough of my attention without trying to raise kids at the same time. I want to be a loving and nurturing parent like my mom was."

Dana stopped paddling and swirled her hand in the cold water. "I wasn't expecting my mom to have a heart attack—she was pretty healthy. I always thought my uncle would die first because he was the one who wasn't well. Doesn't seem fair. Maybe God's punishing him by keeping him alive. He's in an assisted living facility where he has round-the-clock care due to the Alzheimer's he developed when I was a teenager. At least I don't have to worry and wonder if he's hurting anyone else. Sort of a trial-less prison sentence, I guess."

She paused, staring into the distance. "My mother was what kept me going all those years. She didn't know what was happening, but nonetheless she always seemed to put me first. I think that only made my uncle take his anger out on me even more, unfortunately. My uncle was a lot older than my dad, and I think, looking back as an adult, that my uncle had hoped to marry my mother."

"And your mother...?" Luke began hesitantly. "Where was she when your uncle was..." Luke's voice trailed off into silence.

"She worked part-time at night. And, of course, being a little kid, I was afraid of what my uncle would do to me if I told her. I made up excuses for the occasional bruise when he hit me. All I wanted to do was put it out of my mind, anyway, and not think about it." She turned and looked at Luke. "When I was growing up, I didn't want anyone to hug me or kiss me, not even my mother. I kept my feelings to myself, and my greatest regret is how infrequently I told Mom I loved her. I've never been good at expressing my feelings, but I'm working on it."

"Well, I believe expressing yourself through words isn't necessarily what's important," Luke said. "*How* you communicate is what matters, as long as you speak with your heart and listen with your heart. Toward the end, before Jamie died, she couldn't talk. But I understood what she was trying to say by the way she looked at me, the way she squeezed my hand, the expressions on her face. She spoke to me from her heart without needing words."

He smiled gently. "I'm sure your mom knew how you felt about her."

They paddled the rest of the way in silence, each lost in thought. As they rounded the bend toward the house, Sitka stood up from where he had been keeping vigil and ran down to meet them.

After greeting Sitka and storing the kayaks, Luke and Dana changed into their "bathing suits" and climbed into the hot tub for a relaxing soak.

Dana smiled. "This is the life," she said contentedly.

Luke chuckled. "You look like the Cheshire cat."

She touched his arm lightly. "Thank you again for everything you've done for me."

"I haven't done anything," Luke replied, though he had to admit to himself he was pleased she thought he had helped her.

"Yes. You have," Dana insisted. "I don't know whether it's you or the island or both, but I've never been so happy or more at peace."

"It's the hot tub, without a doubt."

Dana laughed. "That too." She gazed at the distant skyline and then turned back to Luke. "For years I tried not to remember what happened. But the only way I could do that was to block almost *all* of my memories. I also had to stop *feeling* anything, because the bad feelings always came with the good—like feeling good and being happy weren't okay.

"But here I haven't needed to keep my feelings under control. And even though I've been trying to feel everything to the fullest, my nightmares have stopped." Dana kept her eyes on Luke's as she hesitantly continued. "And...um, I've been overwhelmed by...by thoughts of you."

Luke wondered if she had actually said the words or if he had just convinced himself that she had.

"I haven't tried to talk myself out of my feelings or deny

them because I am trying so hard to...to let the sensations flow in my body."

Luke struggled to keep his expression passive.

Dana gave a sigh of relief. "There. I've said it. But, um, I don't want you to misunderstand what I'm going to say. You know that I'm planning on...that I have to go home soon. Back to Mark." She fingered the ends of her braids and took a deep breath, holding Luke's gaze. "But I'm finding I'm experiencing sexual desire—for *you*—and for that I am very grateful."

Luke felt his body respond to her words. "Dana—"

"Please, let me finish. When I was young and wasn't able to say no, I had no control. Too late to keep from damaging my relationship with Mark, I realized the only way I could be in control was to say no, especially in a sexual situation. I would think, *When I say no to you, I say yes to myself.* But now I realize I can choose to say yes, just as I can choose to say no. If I *choose* to say yes to my sexuality, I can still be saying yes to myself without denying that part of myself that keeps me from being me."

She reached out to Luke, saying softly, "I have thought about this a lot, and I am not going to deny what I am feeling for you in my body or in my heart."

Luke was sure Dana could hear his heart pounding as he took her hand and admitted, "I've been debating whether to say anything to you, whether it was fair to let you know my feelings."

Dana looked surprised and clasped Luke's hand. "*I'm* the one who's not being fair...to you. Or maybe to me, either. But I need to know if what I'm feeling is real and whether I'm capable of enjoying sex and feeling passion. For the first time in my life, I think I might be able to do that, with you."

Keenly aware of the electricity he felt from her touch, Luke released Dana's hand and stepped out of the hot tub.

He walked to the railing and looked out across the water for a long time.

"Mark?" he asked simply, still facing away from Dana.

"I can't ignore the fact that he's in my life, and of course I don't want to. But I believe—and I think Mark will also come to understand—that this is what I need to do for both of our sakes."

This was what he had dreamed about, wasn't it? Loving her physically in a way that matched his emotional passion for her. Hadn't he been lying awake at night, yearning for just this moment? And the longer she'd stayed, the more he'd allowed himself to hope she would change her mind about Mark and stay with him. Now that that didn't seem possible, what did he really want? Would he—*could* he—be satisfied with just an intimate friendship?

Lost in thought, Luke ran his hands through his hair. He was silent for several long minutes. Finally he turned around and faced Dana, his doubts vanquished and his decision made.

"Since I don't really know what the future holds for you," he said, "I don't really know what the future holds for me. But this is the first time I have felt anything for another woman since Jamie died, and I am grateful to you for that. I didn't think I'd ever be able to love again." Luke's voice was husky with passion. "I want to enjoy whatever time we have together—and enjoy it to the fullest."

He turned abruptly and looked back at the water. "I guess I've had a lot of guilt since Jamie died. She wasn't able to really enjoy the *Warm Breeze* or see this house completed. Before we began construction, I kept saying, 'Let me fish for one more year before we build our home and start our family.' She never complained, just kept waiting patiently." He shook his head ruefully.

"Then she became ill, and too late I realized my priorities had been misplaced."

Dana got out of the hot tub, wrapped a towel around her, and walked to Luke's side.

"Until I met you," he continued, "I'd never met anyone I wanted to get to know better. I've kept to myself, basically staying over here, hanging on to her memory." He faced Dana, taking her hands. "You've helped me to see love is possible again. Even though you're…planning on leaving, I want to know you, in every sense of the word. I don't want to have the regrets I have about Jamie. I don't want to say later on—like I did when Jamie's condition worsened and it became obvious she wouldn't recover—'I wish I had' or 'If only I had.'"

Chapter Eleven

The day had finally faded into twilight. In contrast to the waning light, Dana felt she was seeing clearly for perhaps the first time in her adult life.

Luke held a candle to illuminate their way up the stairs to his loft bedroom. Setting the candle on the small nightstand, he pulled Dana toward him. He cupped Dana's face in his hands and kissed her tenderly. "I will be very gentle. And I will honor and respect your feelings."

Dana's eyes glistened. "Those are the most beautiful words I've ever heard." She wrapped her arms around him and buried her face in his shoulder. Luke's promise was what she had been desperately craving her entire life; it was a balm to her wounds, to her tortured heart and spirit. It wasn't as if Mark had been callous or rough. Quite the contrary, in fact. But she never felt he fully understood the depth of her anguish the way Luke had so immediately.

Tears flowed down Dana's face as she realized this is what she must have sensed in Luke the first time she saw him: that he knew who she was deep in his soul.

Dana had replaced the Disney World shorts and shirt with an oversized T-shirt, which reached halfway to her knees. She lay down on the bed. She looked out the second-story bay window and had the sensation she could almost touch the trees swaying outside.

Luke knelt beside her, stroking her shoulder and whispering her name. She rolled over and looked into his eyes for reassurance. He repeated his soothing words of reverence, and her heart overflowed with love.

Still, Dana was very nervous, and she was sure Luke knew that. As much as she trusted him and wanted to feel him deep inside her, she didn't know if she could really go through with it. She felt as if she were a virgin all over again, as if this would be the first time and as the first time should be.

"Turn over, and I'll rub your back," he said gently.

Luke's voice caressed her, and Dana began to relax. He carefully reached under her T-shirt and began rubbing her shoulders and back. His touch was firm yet tender—and very sensuous.

"Is this okay?" he asked quietly.

"Oh, yes," Dana murmured, luxuriating in his touch.

Luke kissed the back of her neck so lightly Dana almost wasn't sure if his lips were actually touching her. He then turned her over, gently removing her T-shirt. He spoke soothingly and lovingly as he did so, obviously wanting his quiet words to put her at ease.

"You're so beautiful," Luke said. He stood and quickly undressed, letting his clothes fall in a heap on the floor.

He lay beside her and kissed her tenderly while slowly and gently stroking her body, responding in kind to her responses to his touch. He buried his hand in her hair. "Look into my eyes, Dana. Remember you're with *me*."

Dana returned his kisses, focusing on the new sensations that were flowing through her body. As they pressed against each other, she unconsciously spread her legs in invitation. As Luke gently pushed inside her, holding her gaze with his own, a profound sense of well-being enveloped Dana, and she knew she was doing the right thing. Their passion swelled. She arched her back and pulled him deeper, trembling with desire and need.

Without warning, she stiffened. Was she ready for this? She tried to concentrate on Luke, on the exquisite feelings surging through her body, and on keeping her mental demons at bay, but she kept seeing her uncle. The bliss and, yes, hunger she had felt moments ago had vanished. She became distracted and afraid. She was going to get hurt. She always did.

Luke sensed the change in her and stopped. In a hushed voice, he said, "Dana. Stay with me. I'm not your uncle. Love *me*."

His words brought her back, and she relaxed. Tenderly they resumed their lovemaking.

Dana screwed her eyes shut and repeated silently, *It's okay to love. Love doesn't have to hurt.* Her fears melted away as she immersed herself in Luke. Their movements became one, and she was carried away on a wave of increasing sexual passion.

"Feel it, Dana," Luke whispered urgently. "Let yourself go. You can do it. Feeling like this is okay."

But her uncle's face loomed larger, and despite great effort, Dana couldn't block him out. She heard his slurring voice saying, "I love you. That's why I'm doing this. You won't ever be able to enjoy this when you get older. Any other man who wants to do this will hurt you. And if you ever tell anyone about this, they'll be disgusted by you. They won't be able to love you. I'm the only one who will love you."

Abruptly Dana pulled away from Luke and curled into a ball. She couldn't bear to face him. Why had she thought she could do this? "I'm sorry. I can't. I just can't."

Luke grabbed a light blanket and covered her, then gently kissed her cheek. "It's okay, Dana. Just know that I love you."

Luke's words made Dana cry. She turned toward him, clutching his hand. Tears ran from one eye to the other, pooling on the pillow. Luke gathered her into his arms, stroking her hair, murmuring his love for her.

Dana nestled against him, her agonizing memories gradually seeping from her body. She fell asleep wrapped in his protective embrace.

Sometime later she awoke to darkness—a darkness in the depths of her being as well as in the sky. Why had she thought this time would be any different? Would there ever be a time when her uncle's voice didn't haunt her—and taunt her—when she tried to make love?

She was lying on her right side, her legs curled slightly, and Luke's body was wrapped around her. Though his chest was pressed against her back, she could feel their hearts touching. Luke's quiet words of love replayed in her mind. The warmth that had been in his voice and the tenderness of his caresses gradually melted her despair. He *had* honored her and respected her, and she knew his love and strength would protect her. Optimism replaced desperation, and she once again fell asleep in Luke's sheltering arms.

The next day was blustery and cool. For once Sitka stayed indoors, enjoying the warmth of the fire. Neither Dana nor Luke mentioned the night before. Luke taught Dana five-card stud. She learned quickly, and at twenty-five cents a chip, by late afternoon was ahead by twenty dollars.

"Enough," Luke finally announced. He held up his hands in defeat. "Are you sure you've never played poker before?"

"Nope." Dana arranged her chips in neat piles. "Never."

"Amazing. Must be beginner's luck." Luke smiled. "I'd love to see you in a game with Jake."

"He collects shells, grows flowers, and plays poker too?" Dana returned Luke's smile. "No wonder women are crazy about him."

"Yeah. And he cooks too. Taught me how to barbecue those ribs we had the other night."

"They were delicious," Dana said. "Glad we have some left over for tonight."

After a late dinner, they took Sitka on a walk. Sitka looked back frequently, apparently wanting to make sure they were following him. They strolled in companionable silence until they reached the rock bridge.

"What's winter like here?" Dana finally asked.

Luke skirted a fallen tree and pushed aside a large devil's club leaf in Dana's path. "Well...wild and wonderful. So much happens quietly. I like to watch the snow being swirled around by shifting winds, landing on the boughs of the trees. Sometimes thick flakes settle on everything like a blanket. The air is heavy, muffling every sound."

Sitka suddenly veered off to chase a squirrel and was soon swallowed up by the dense foliage.

"The weather can change dramatically," Luke continued. "One day it might be ten degrees and snowing, the next, thirty-five and raining. Sometimes even in January, the promise of spring is in the air. When the days are noticeably longer in early February, everyone's spirits lift." He smiled. "Even Sitka's."

They crossed the rock bridge and sat down by the point. Dana was suddenly overwhelmed by the same feelings she had experienced as a little girl, when she was desperate to be safe, to be comforted, and to be touched without being hurt. She took a deep breath and faced Luke, yet again grateful for his calming presence. If only she could tell him everything.

"You know, I'm not *supposed* to have wonderful feelings about sex." Dana picked at the moss.

"What do you mean?" Luke's surprise was obvious. "Of course you are."

"No, I'm not," she said, shaking her head.

"Yes, you are," Luke persisted.

"*No, I'm not.*" Dana was vehement. "And I'm having trouble convincing myself otherwise."

"Why?"

"Because he said…my uncle said…if I couldn't enjoy what *he* did to me, I wouldn't *ever* be able to enjoy it. He made sure of it too. He did so many horrible things to me that…"

She shivered, and Luke put his arm around her. "Smells like rain," he said.

Dana nodded. "Look at that sky."

The sky to the north was black with an impending storm. A few rays of the setting sun were still visible through the broken clouds hanging over the mountain range to the west. A lone seagull flew across the backdrop of the threatening sky. Dana noticed Luke's gaze was also drawn to the contrast between the black sky and the white bird. As they watched, the last beam of sunshine spotlighted the gull, illuminating it a blazing white. The seagull continued its journey across the darkened sky, looking like an angel.

"Remember, Dana," Luke said. "*Anything* is possible."

The summer storm blew up, and all night the wind raged, mirroring Dana's emotions. Each time she and Luke began making love, she would soon pull away and curl into a tight ball, her back to him, holding her stuffed bear as if her life depended on it. Though she tried to concentrate on the present, on Luke's palpable love for her, the past gripped her like a vise. And each time she ended up facing the window and crying softly, watching the swaying trees, listening to the pelting rain and the waves crashing against the rocks, praying for a miracle.

Chapter Twelve

THE NEXT MORNING DAWNED CLEAR AND FRESH, AND AS ON THE previous morning, nothing about the night before was said over breakfast. While Luke washed the dishes, Dana sipped on a mug of hot tea. Feeling restless, she got up and walked to one of the large front windows, her mind swirling.

I'm safe here. I trust Luke. He cherishes me. Why can't I let go of those feelings from the past?

She opened the door to let Sitka outside and breathed deeply. The air smelled fresher than ever. The colors seemed more vibrant. Suddenly she knew with clarity what she had to do. She *had* to tell him. Every last detail. It was her only hope.

She turned. "Luke, I think I need to tell you...the rest." Without waiting for a reply, Dana walked onto the deck.

Luke put down the bowl he was washing and followed her. He leaned against the railing, saying nothing.

Dana suddenly felt a bit uncertain. "I don't actually know how to say this." Anxiously, she brushed a strand of hair away from her face. Before Luke could respond, she continued, "I've never told this to anyone, not even Mark." She paced and tugged nervously on her braids. Would he recoil from her once he knew the truth? Was she taking too big a chance?

"Why aren't there any mosquitoes over here?" Dana asked. "I didn't think any place in Alaska was free of mosquitoes."

"My guess is because there's no source of fresh water on the island. That's why I collect rainwater."

"Oh."

"Dana..." Luke paused. "I'm guessing you're avoiding the subject. You don't need to tell me."

"Yes, I do. When you say truths out loud, you can't deny their existence anymore. You have to face them." She stopped pacing but continued wringing her hands.

"When we make love, or rather I should say, when we *begin* to, I can't stop seeing..." Dana let out an anguished moan.

"Are you sure you want to tell me?" Luke asked again.

"Yes. I have to." She took a deep breath and started again, feeling like she was putting her future—her life—in his hands. But she knew with certainty she had to continue. "I tried to say no to my uncle many times. One day I did, and he threatened me with a gun. He pointed it at my head and said he'd kill me if I didn't do what he wanted. Then he pulled the trigger—and it clicked. It was empty. No bullets. *Too bad,* I remember thinking. *That would have solved everything.*

"I continued to resist, and things got worse. Sometimes he put the gun in my mouth. Sometimes he shoved the gun inside me. And sometimes he'd throw me down into the cellar, slam the door shut and lock it, leaving me in the darkness with all the creepy, crawly things a young child imagined were brushing up against her."

She stole a glance at Luke. He had a look of sheer horror on his face.

"I'm not sure what was worse, the pain of what he did or the total isolation I felt. There was no one to help me or to talk to. I was desperate for someone to come charging out of nowhere and save me, like in the fairy tales.

"In the months before my eighth birthday, he started telling me he was going to kill me on my birthday if I kept resisting him. I had a dog named Boots. He was my best friend. I think he even protected me a couple of times—growled just loud enough when my uncle was just tired enough that he gave up and left me alone." Her voice was filled with sadness as she added, "One day I came home from school, and my uncle had arranged to have him put to sleep."

"That's terrible!"

"So, even at seven, I could comprehend my own death. That this man could kill me. If he could do that to Boots…I told my friends not to come to my birthday party because I didn't think I'd be there.

"Then, in the early morning of my birthday, while my mom was still at work"— Dana paused and stared into the distance, seeing it happen all over again, like watching a movie—"he carried me outside to my playhouse. He stripped off my clothes and then laid me in my old cradle, which I used for my dolls. The cradle was pretty big, and I still almost fit into it. Then he took my jump rope and tied my arms together over my chest so I couldn't fight him off."

Dana spoke so softly, Luke had to lean forward to hear her appalling words.

Her tears flowed unchecked. "He put the gun to my head and told me he loved me. He said he was sorry he was going to have to kill me, but if he couldn't have me, no one could.

"I kept hoping for that knight in shining armor to appear in the nick of time and rescue me. Until finally I gave up hoping and felt it would be a blessing if I died. No more torture. No more pain. No more acting. I begged and pleaded with my uncle to do it. 'Kill me, please! Kill me and get it over with!' But then, just as suddenly, he lowered the gun, untied the rope, and walked out of the playhouse without a word.

"He never touched me again."

Luke stared at Dana in obvious shock, the muscles twitching in his face revealing his inner rage. "Dana, I—"

Gently Dana touched Luke's arm. She understood the enormity of what she had just told him would be difficult to absorb. "Long ago I acknowledged these things had happened to me. But we can't change the past. What I want and need is to make peace with it, to let go of the pain, to move on and find a way to live my life fully."

Luke was clearly struggling to contain his anger for Dana's sake. "That anyone could do that to you is inconceivable. That it was your own uncle is sickening and horrifying—beyond words. You've suffered enough for several lifetimes." He clenched his fists. "I'd like to kill him."

Dana took hold of his hands, as much for her sake as his. "Hearing that really helps." She sighed deeply. "Somehow I found the strength to keep going. My mom remarried, my uncle moved out, and soon I locked my memories away. Both my mom and my stepdad encouraged me to be anything I wanted to be, and surprisingly, I ended up with a lot of self-confidence, though obviously not as far as men are concerned.

"I managed to keep the abuse out of my mind until Mark and I had been together for a while, as I said. When my sexual problems surfaced along with the memories, I couldn't ignore what had happened to me. Lately, the things my uncle did to me on my birthday and with the gun have become recurring nightmares. Except here, on your island." *With you.*

"And you never confronted him about this?" Luke's face still registered shock.

"No. What's important to me is the present, not the past, and that's what I have to focus on. Anyway, since he's now suffering from Alzheimer's, it's a moot point. Over the years, though, I've filled notebook after notebook with my feelings and thoughts. Just as building your home was your salvation, writing has been mine. I don't need to confront my uncle. I need to confront myself."

Dana awoke from a late-afternoon nap to the aroma of barbecued salmon. She opened her eyes and grinned. Sitka was keeping vigil at the Weber, hoping for a tidbit.

She sat up and stretched. "How did you know that's how I like salmon the best?" she asked Luke.

"Lucky guess." Luke upended his bottle of beer and finished it in one swallow. "Would you like some wine with dinner?"

"I would, thanks. You know, all these years I've had an aversion to drinking and being around people who drink. Guess that's easy to figure out: my uncle had always been drinking when he came to my room, and the drunker he was, the more violent he was. But here I am, actually enjoying an occasional drink."

Luke smiled. "I'm glad you feel relaxed enough here to just be you."

"Well, I'm wondering what's next."

Luke's smile widened. "I know what I'm hoping will be next."

Dana returned his smile and blushed simultaneously. "Do you need any help with dinner?"

"Nope. Everything's under control." He wiped his hands and then reached for his guitar. "I've been thinking about how to get across my thoughts and feelings about the things you've told me and...well, I wrote a song for you."

"Really?" She was touched.

Luke strummed a few chords. "Now, relax—and enjoy..."

Luke's voice was clear and rich; his words expressed pain and sorrow along with the calmness of acceptance and the promise of a new beginning. The song profoundly touched Dana, bringing her both a sense of contentment and a whisper of hope.

When Luke set aside his guitar, Dana pressed her hand to her heart, deeply moved. Her eyes were filled with tears. "That was...so beautiful. Thank you."

Overcome, she put her head on his shoulder and wept. She prayed the next time they made love would be different but feared it would only be worse.

Later that night, after dinner, Luke was even more gentle and understanding when they made love. His voice was calming and reassuring. He tried to distract Dana from her thoughts and so overwhelm her with his love that she would concentrate only on what she was feeling. The moment he sensed her body was tensing and she was about to pull away, he stopped touching her, knowing she was fighting for her life, lost in her own world, a hell he could not imagine. Trying to help destroy her living nightmare, he focused his thoughts on her, willing her pain to disappear.

At the same time he wondered...was she remembering what it felt like to be lying naked in her cradle, her arms tied across her chest—with her own jump rope, for God's sake? Was she remembering the feel of the gun in her mouth, the sound of the gun being cocked, and then finally begging her own uncle to kill her? Was she remembering being thrown into that frightening cellar? Staying there in complete darkness, until once again she gave in to his twisted demands?

Abruptly Dana rolled onto her right side, facing the window and curling into a fetal position. Not wanting to intrude on her thoughts, but still offer support, Luke placed his arm around her, hoping his presence was of some comfort.

As the twilight faded into darkness, Luke could hear Dana's breathing slow down. Soon she was asleep, clutching her worn stuffed animal. Luke whispered to her, from his heart, repeatedly assuring her of his love and respect for her, sentiments that were paramount to both of them.

The next day, Dana spent most of her time with Sitka. They explored the tide pools and sunned themselves on the rocks. She frequently pulled out a folded piece of paper from the back pocket of her jeans and read it aloud: "I am an adult now, not a child. He can't hurt me anymore."

Those words were juxtaposed in her mind with thoughts of Luke and everything he meant to her. The sheltering aura that emanated from him was tangible, offering a refuge she had hungered for. She prayed she would soon be able to finally purge the darkness within her, as well as the secrets, that had kept her from integrating her fragmented heart and body into a complete whole.

She gathered strength from these meditations, and gradually despair was once again replaced by hope.

That evening, after a long soak in the hot tub, Dana fell asleep on Luke's bed with a towel wrapped loosely around her naked body. When Luke climbed in bed beside her, she stirred awake and turned toward him. The shell he had given her rolled out from under her pillow, and he set it on the window ledge.

Luke stroked her face gently, murmuring, "I won't let anything happen to you, Dana. I love you." He then kissed her gently, reverently, and told her, "Remember, anything is possible."

Dana smiled. "I had the best sleep I've had in a long time."

"Shhhh, don't say anything. Just relax and enjoy what you're feeling." And Luke kissed her again.

This time will be different, Dana thought with conviction as Luke ran his fingers up one side of her leg and down the other. *I can do this. I want to do this. I need to do this.* She kept repeating to herself, *It's okay to love. It's okay to feel sensuous and wonderfully alive.*

Luke's lips were warm and inviting.

I have nothing to fear. He can't hurt me anymore.

Dana gave a small moan of desire and welcomed Luke's probing tongue in her mouth. She concentrated on the pleasure he was giving her and refused to let any images of her uncle intrude.

What's holding me back? Luke knows everything about me. And he still loves me. And honors me. She looked deeply into Luke's eyes, feeling overwhelming trust. *You were wrong, Uncle. This man still loves me!*

Suddenly Dana responded to Luke with an intensity she had never even dreamed was possible. Completely relaxed, she was yielding, giving, kissing and touching him everywhere, greedily exploring his body. Every nerve was alive with desire. All the passion she had denied herself was unlocked in one fiery explosion.

She begged him to enter her, and when he did, she cried out with joy and whispered in wonder, "Thank you, God, this doesn't hurt." This time she did not pull away. This time she learned what it was to truly love and be loved.

Stepping onto the deck the next morning, Dana was awestruck, as if she had removed a filter from her camera lens that had dimmed the spectacular beauty of her surroundings. The sky now seemed a deeper blue and the flowers astonishingly vivid; a blissful serenity permeated her entire body.

She had never before felt this depth of peace or this alive; it was as though the intensity of her physical connection with Luke had intensified her senses. She didn't feel alone anymore, and she never wanted to leave.

Part Three

Chapter Thirteen

The minutes melted into hours, the hours into days. Dana and Luke were totally absorbed in each other, and time lost all significance. What was turning out to be an unusually hot late summer for Southcentral Alaska was matched by their passion. For the first time in her life, Dana understood what it meant to make love. Luke helped her to push away her demons, and she experienced new and exhilarating sensations. Her fears dissolved, and they couldn't get enough of each other.

"See what you've done?" Dana periodically asked, laughing. "You've turned me into a sex maniac!"

"Are you sure it isn't the other way around?" Luke would counter, kissing her before she could say anything else.

Dana was an early riser; Luke wasn't. She liked to get up in the mornings, play a soothing CD, and brew her favorite tea, ginger peach. Then, Sitka padding quietly behind her, she would take her mug to one of the many wide window ledges in the house and sip her tea, feeling as if she were floating above the water on a bed of spruce trees. Until her need to be with Luke would overwhelm her, and then she would crawl back into bed, pressing her naked body to his, exploring him with her fingers and her mouth. They always made love slowly in the mornings, gently and tenderly, and when they were locked into each other, they looked deeply into each other's eyes and their hearts joined.

Dana quickly lost her shyness in front of Luke and would spend long hours playing the piano, sometimes composing her own songs. She was enthralled by the beauty and serenity of the world around her. She loved to sit at the piano in the early evening when the sun streamed through the windows. The oblique rays would highlight the golden color of the cedar walls surrounding her, spreading warmth throughout the spacious room and causing the ivory keys to glow as if lit from within.

At low tide one afternoon, Dana and Sitka explored the tide pool pockets in the rocky shoreline in front of the house. It was hot and sunny, the wind was calm—unusual for the late afternoon—and the rocks radiated the sun's warmth.

Dana found a relatively flat rock and brushed away the loose pebbles, grateful yet again for the lack of mosquitoes on the island. Sitka chose a spot nearby. "I think I'll soak up some of this glorious sunshine, Sitka. Sound okay to you?"

She stretched out, closed her eyes, and basked in the sun, the heat warming her face and relaxing her body. The waves were hushed as they broke against the rocks, adding to the tranquility.

Dana was just dozing off when a loud sound broke the stillness. She *knew* that sound: a whale taking a breath! Her drowsiness instantly gone, she bolted upright and caught a glimpse of an orca just as it dove. It surfaced twice more, heading up the bay.

"You're so lucky to live here, Sitka," Dana said, rubbing his ears. Sitka wagged his tail in response, rolled over on his back, and presented his belly for scratching. "I love you, Sitka," Dana murmured, her fingers digging through his thick, warm fur. Sitka closed his eyes and extended his back leg at her touch. "I'm going to miss you, sweet boy." As she lay down to enjoy more of the sun's healing rays, guitar music floated toward her. "I'm going to miss your 'dad,' too. Almost more than I can bear."

Dana sighed deeply. She had lost herself in Luke. She would have to leave soon or she would never be able to. Reluctantly she admitted to herself she had fallen deeply in love with Luke. She had initially dismissed her growing feelings for him as gratitude, working hard to convince herself she was mistaking what she was feeling. She told herself over and over she loved Mark, and whatever she was feeling for Luke would fade once he was no longer in her life.

Yet she really wondered if she would feel differently about Luke when she got home, into Mark's waiting arms. Would these few weeks with Luke seem like just a beautiful dream, a unique moment in time with a very special man in an extraordinary place, a gift in a different reality that couldn't be duplicated elsewhere—even with Luke? How would she ever know? And how much of what she felt was the magic of the island? How much was Luke? Most important, how much was a matter of her facing and letting go of the past?

As she sat up, she told herself Mark's desire for her had never waned. Even when they were struggling as a couple, she believed in his love. And she was optimistic she could now return it. Mark was steadfast, unconditional, and patient. She loved him, and she couldn't imagine life without him. She felt an urgent need to explain to him what had happened on her eighth birthday and what it all meant, what everything that had happened to her as a child meant. She wanted to tell him, and show him, she could now enjoy a man—him—touching her body.

Dana was so wrapped up in her thoughts, she didn't hear Luke approach. She only became aware of his presence when he kissed her gently on the back of her neck. Her heart filled, and she turned and smiled at him, pushing her concerns and worries away.

A few days later Luke asked, "What do you say we take the *Warm Breeze* up the bay and stay overnight?"

"That would be wonderful!"

They quickly gathered the supplies and clothes they would need and made their way out to the sailboat. There was just enough wind to fill the sails, and the water was lightly rippled as they left the island behind them. Luke let out the mainsail on the starboard side. He then fastened the whisker pole to the mast, attaching the jib and letting it out on the port side so they could run downwind, wing on wing.

"Keep her on this course while I check a few things," Luke instructed her as he prepared to go below and retrieve a chart for the local area.

Dana took the wheel. "How am I doing?" she asked, beaming, when Luke returned.

"Perfect."

He came up behind her, put his arms around her, and covered her hands with his, pressing his body into hers and nestling his face in her hair to breathe in her scent. Every nerve in Dana's body came alive with his closeness, and she felt she was radiating sensuality. She turned her face toward his and kissed his neck.

How was she ever going to leave?

Yet how could she stay?

She sighed, turning back to face the bow.

They were approaching a small, secluded cove. "This looks good to me. Let's anchor here," Luke suggested.

"*Everywhere* we go looks good. It's all so beautiful," Dana murmured. She snapped a few photos of Luke as he lowered the anchor over the side. The sight of his lean, muscular body stirred hers anew. She felt herself tingling with desire.

Smiling to herself, she put down her camera and asked, "Would you like some coffee?"

"Coffee would be great."

"Okay. Back in a jiff." Dana hurried down the companionway to the galley and made a couple of cups of coffee as quickly as she could. Then she peeled off all of her clothes and made her way back to the deck.

Luke grinned lasciviously as Dana emerged stark naked from the cabin. He grabbed his coffee mug and drank, yelping when he burned his tongue in his haste. Dana eyed him over the rim of her mug, enjoying his obvious hunger for her.

Silently he sauntered over to Dana, took their mugs, and stowed them. Then he tossed off his clothes, grabbed a cushion from the cockpit locker, and threw it down on the deck. Dana lay down eagerly, reaching out to him. She immediately lost herself in their mutual passion and refused to think about the future.

It was a beautiful evening, clear and warm. After a late dinner, they piled into the dinghy—Sitka included—and rowed to shore, where they built a fire and enjoyed the solitude. Sitka curled up next to Dana and was soon asleep.

While Luke went to find more wood for the fire, Dana focused on the soft sounds that filled the night: Sitka's measured breathing, the gentle breeze rustling through the trees, a loon calling in the distance, the crackling fire, her own heartbeat. As she watched Luke, her heart beat faster. Unquestionably and absolutely, he drove her wild with desire. He carried her to levels of sexual pleasure she had not even imagined were possible, satisfying the inner reaches of both body and spirit.

Suddenly her chest constricted with anxiety. Would she really be able to respond to Mark in the same way? What would she do if she couldn't?

Luke returned and tossed several pieces of driftwood on the fire. "That ought to be enough," he said. Flames crackled, and sparks spit into the sky. He sat beside Dana and put his arm around her, pulling her close. "Beautiful night, isn't it?"

Quickly pulling herself together, Dana replied, "Mmmmm, yes. My grandparents used to make bonfires like this on their beach. I looked forward to those vacations more than anything." She pulled her knees to her chest and stared into the fire. "Every morning I would sit at the tide pools for hours, before anyone else was on the beach. I loved the crash of the waves on the rocks. I'd look out into the vastness of the sea and sit close enough to the water's edge to feel the spray. The ocean always soothed me. It was my refuge."

She kissed him tenderly on his cheek. "Just as you and your island have soothed me and given me refuge. I want you to know when I was finally able to relax and truly enjoy sex with you, I wanted to make love with you out of desire. I guess what I'm trying to say is I didn't *need* to—as a means of finally expelling the bad memories—I *wanted* to. As a matter of fact"—Dana shifted and kissed Luke gently on the lips—"I see that as a big step. I am consumed by passion, not by the past. Being able to lose myself in you and experience uncontrollable sexual desire is, well"—Dana blushed before continuing—"wonderful and gives me strength. Hopefully, I can look back at my past from a distance, as a different person—"

"You *are* a different person, Dana," Luke said, touching her cheek.

Dana stared at Luke. He was right. She *was* different. She didn't need love to hurt anymore, and she was able to offer herself to Luke totally and completely. By surrendering herself, trusting herself to let go, she received much more than she gave. As well as experiencing exquisite sexual pleasure and release, she connected to her inner self in a way she had long denied. Her pain and suffering were replaced by peace, serenity, and calm—words that had only been words before. Her despair of ever knowing passion with Mark was replaced by hope. She nodded. "I used to think you were healed first and then serenity just happened. But now I see that by letting go of the past, serenity takes over and heals.

"I can look back at my childhood now, and it doesn't reach out and grab me. Many times before, I thought I had reached that place, but then something unexpected would happen. I'd read an article or watch a news clip on child abuse, and my own abuse would come back to haunt me again. Like a scab ripped off a healing wound, the trauma was once again exposed. I know I won't forget the past, and occasionally something will remind me of it, but I don't think it will ever control me again. *I am in control. Of my mind *and* my body.*"

Luke cupped Dana's face in his hands and kissed her deeply. "And what a beautiful body you have," he whispered.

Dana smiled. She wasn't ashamed anymore.

She pressed her body against his and gave in to her own passion.

Dana awoke and peered through the cabin's small porthole. The sky was just beginning to lighten. Luke was still sleeping beside her, and she gazed at his body and thought about the exquisite pleasure he gave her. Sighing deeply and wondering once again how in the world she was going to leave, Dana climbed out of the bunk and tiptoed up the companionway to find Sitka waiting for her on deck. She helped Sitka into the dinghy and rowed them to shore. Sitka jumped into the shallow water on the beach and began exploring the tide line.

Dana followed Sitka, enjoying his exuberance, and then returned to the spot where she and Luke had built the fire the night before. And where they had yet again made love. She looked out to the *Warm Breeze,* scanning the deck for a sign of Luke. She decided he must still be asleep below and searched for perfect skimming rocks so she could challenge him to a stone-skipping contest later. Maybe this time she'd let him win.

She couldn't stop thinking about Luke. Serendipitously, she had found sanctuary with this extraordinary man and had welcomed him into her soul. So many years ago, sexual acts had created fear, revulsion, and the certainty that love hurts. The unbearable feeling she'd frequently had in her arms, reliving the sensation of having her arms tied together with her jump rope, had finally disappeared, replaced by loving, caring, exciting embraces. Now her arms felt light, almost buoyant, as if they were floating in a sea of well-being and happiness, finally unburdened and free from the horrific restraints of her past.

She closed her eyes and felt Luke's love for her penetrating her, flowing through her body, reaching every nerve. What a remarkably sensual man! He brought out a side of her she hadn't known existed, hadn't known *could* exist. She never stopped marveling at how she felt when she was around him. Just thinking about him caused intense desire to smolder within her until it quickly burst into a fiery and uncontrollable passion. Feeling safe, feeling cherished, feeling whole when they made love was what had been, and would always be, so liberating for her.

Dana looked at the *Warm Breeze* again just as Luke appeared on deck. She waved. How she would treasure the time they had spent together! Whistling for Sitka, she turned and walked back along the shore to the dinghy and shoved it into the water. After Sitka jumped in, she rowed back to the sailboat, watching the small cove, which reminded her of the one on Luke's island, grow farther and farther away.

Chapter Fourteen

THE NEXT DAY WAS COOL AND RAINY, SO DANA AND LUKE SPENT the day indoors, much of it enjoying the warmth of the fire. Afternoon found Dana curled up in a large beanbag chair, writing. Sitka was, as usual, asleep at her feet. Luke sat across from them, tying sailors' knots.

He looked over and smiled. "Looks like you've got another notebook almost filled up. You'll have that bestseller done in no time!"

Dana returned Luke's smile. "Who knows? Maybe I *will* write a book someday." She studied his handiwork. "That knot you're working on is very intricate. What's it called?"

"A Turk's head. Hundreds of years ago, sailors perfected these knots on their long sea voyages." Luke held up the length of line he was braiding, eyeing it critically. "This one, which has a quadrangular center, takes considerable concentration."

"I think I missed the macramé era," Dana said. "I'll leave that to you mariners." She glanced at her watch; it was almost five. "I haven't listened to the bushlines since yesterday morning."

Luke nodded. "Yeah, I suppose we should catch up on the news as well."

Dana leaned over to the minimal stereo equipment that rested on a lower bookshelf and clicked the knob on the radio. "Although what's happening elsewhere doesn't seem to matter much here. It's easy to forget another world exists."

She turned up the volume. The daily classical hour had just ended, and the five o'clock news began. After thirty minutes of national, state, and local news, the broadcaster announced, "And now it's time for the bushlines.

"To Pete and Annie at the cove. Meet me at 5:00 p.m. on Sunday. Same place as before. I promise I'll be on time. From Lucy.

"To Charlie and Sharon at the lagoon. Had a great time. Thanks for everything. See you in Anchorage next week. From Jane and Randy."

Dana was so focused on Luke's knot tying, admiring the skillful way he crisscrossed the strands of thin line, she almost missed her name.

"To Dana across the bay."

She and Luke both froze and stared at the radio. Dana felt her heart stop.

"I miss you. Hope things are going well. I love you. And that's from Mark."

Dana felt stricken. She stood up and walked slowly to the large front window, where she stared outside, unseeing.

Luke was quiet. After a few moments he said, "Dana, I'll understand if you want to..." His voice trailed off into the uncomfortable silence that filled the expanse.

"I think I need some fresh air," she finally managed to say. "I won't be gone long. I know it's my turn to cook dinner."

"Don't worry about that. We have plenty of leftovers. I'll heat up something. No need to hurry back."

Dana looked gratefully at Luke and put on her raincoat. Sitka followed her outside. Although she had always known she would have to return to Mark, she hadn't been prepared to actually face the reality of her leaving. Now she couldn't ignore it any longer.

She walked until she found a fairly dry spot under a large spruce. Sitting down on the spongy moss, Dana buried her face in Sitka's fur and hugged him tightly while she cried.

Three more days passed. The early-morning sun was shining through the loft's bay window, casting long, golden rays on Dana and Luke's entwined bodies. The delicate flutelike sound of the hermit thrush sounded clear in the stillness.

Dana couldn't sleep. She felt the sound of Luke's voice caressing her, soft and smooth as velvet. She thought of his kisses brushing the inside of her thighs, fanning the fire that burned inside her. She pressed against him, imagining he was entering her. She almost climaxed as she closed her eyes, actually feeling the pleasure he gave her. Her newfound sensuality came from within her, but Luke was most assuredly the key that had unlocked an almost insatiable desire to feel more, learn more, enjoy more, and try anything and everything. Spontaneous and uninhibited, she now thoroughly enjoyed her body instead of recoiling from it.

Touching her fingers to his chest, she kissed him on the lips. It took all of her self-control to keep from running her hands up and down his body, caressing him with her fingertips. But she decided she would let him sleep as long as he wanted. She carefully disentangled herself from his embrace and slipped off the bed, dressing quickly. Sitka stirred when she did and followed her down the spiral staircase. They went out on the deck, and Dana leaned against the railing, breathing in the freshness after last night's rain.

"Ready for our morning walk, Sitka?" Dana asked.

Hearing the word *walk*, Sitka bounded down the steps from the deck and raced along the trail well ahead of her.

When Dana caught up, he was already lying on the mossy point of the rock bridge. She sat down with him and took out her notebook.

I sit and think of nothing. Or maybe it's everything…seeping in, like the tide, then gradually receding, leaving traces in the sand. What remains? Memories, feelings, conversations all jumbled up together. I am a blank page, allowing only what I want to become the script for my life, discarding what has troubled me, keeping what now forms the outline of the person I'm becoming, the person that I am. Me.

Dana looked up, her thoughts racing, matching the clouds moving double time across the sky as if in time-lapse photography. The fireweed was at its peak. First in town and then here, she had watched the beautiful dark-pink blossoms work their way from the bottom to the top of the upper stem. The flowers would soon go to seed, and fall would be in the air. She remembered what Luke had said: "When the first fireweed blossoms begin to bloom and cover the hillsides, summer is at its height. But the flowers are a mixed blessing because they mean summer's about to end. When the last blossoms bloom at the top of the plant, the first frost is only six weeks away."

She knew what she had to do, as difficult as it was going to be. It was time to return home and feel things all over again for the first time, as a new woman with a new life. She owed it to Mark and to herself. She had been reluctant to marry Mark when she couldn't love him in every sense, with all of her body as well as all of her heart. She had learned to let go of her defenses, to surrender herself and to trust another, allowing her to know incredible joy in a physical relationship. All these years she should have been letting go instead of trying to forget. She now understood that when you finally let something go, you still remember it, but it gradually fades from dominance. Yet the big question remained: could she love Mark the way she loved Luke? And there was only one way to find out.

Stowing her notebook in her backpack, Dana stood and gazed off the point. Sitka nuzzled her hand, and as she petted him, Dana reflected how different she was from the person she'd been when she first saw him standing on the deck of the *Warm Breeze*. Now she was confident, happy, and incredibly alive. Those two people who had battled within her had finally integrated and become one.

In a moment of panic, she worried how Mark would react to the changes that had occurred in her. After living within a set of behavior patterns that had never varied, would Mark be able to adjust to her new sense of self? Despite the sexual problems they had had, would he wish she was still the woman he had fallen in love with? Maybe he preferred the way she used to be, when she wasn't capable of deep feelings and was usually compliant with his wishes, just content to be with someone who loved her and accepted her past—at least as much as she had told him—regardless of the impact it had had on her. Had she changed so much they wouldn't fit anymore? She fervently hoped Mark would be able to cherish her for who she was today, not who she used to be, and rejoice in her new inner strength, independence, and sense of self, as well as her new sensuality.

With sudden clarity and certainty, Dana realized she would have to tell Mark about Luke. She didn't know how else she could describe the dynamic changes within her, the reasons for those changes, and the new person she had become. Whatever the outcome, the years of harboring secrets were over.

Reluctantly Dana started back, knowing she needed to leave this blissful sanctuary and determine her future. As she and Sitka walked slowly though the island, she focused on the sights and sounds around her, memorizing every detail. A squirrel chattered, and Sitka, unfailingly optimistic, bounded off to chase it. From a high point on the island, the lush vegetation spread out below her in a sea of tall ferns and broad devil's club leaves canopied by majestic trees. Dana knew she hadn't been able to capture the essence of the island with her camera. That, along with her memories of Luke, would have to remain within her heart.

Luke. Would she ever see him again? Her newfound happiness and peace were heavy with heartache, but she couldn't let that mar her final hours with him. She needed to concentrate on the love and joy they shared, not the pain of saying good-bye.

When she got back to the house, she found him sitting on the small deck by the hot tub, strumming his guitar. The harmonious sounds were moving and very beautiful, mirroring the story of their love, friendship, and impending separation. Luke stopped playing when Dana approached.

He studied her before saying, "You're leaving, aren't you?" His voice was filled with sadness.

Dana nodded. "Tomorrow."

Luke opened his mouth to speak but swallowed his reply.

"Mark has always been there for me. Even before we became a couple, he was a loyal friend." Dana desperately wanted him to understand. "When I was young, I couldn't tell him what had happened. I'd show up at my grandparents' for a visit, and I was so relieved to be away from home that generally I was happy. But sometimes Mark would find me alone and crying. He never pried, just asked if there was anything he could do. I think that's when I decided I would love him forever."

She paused and wiped away a tear.

"Anyway, I always brushed off his concern, and we'd scramble down the cliff to the beach to spend hours playing in the sand, building sand castles, beachcombing, running with his dog.

"When I finally told him what my uncle did to me, I told him everything that had happened, except that my uncle had threatened to kill me. Acknowledging to anyone else that he wanted to kill me would be admitting I wasn't worth anything. If my own uncle didn't want me around, what other man would?"

Her tears spilled over. "Up to now, I could never allow myself to love Mark the way I love you. Even before my mom died and the painful memories came flooding back, I could never really let myself go and just...feel...in my heart and in my body, without the past squashing those feelings. All these years I've never really known how to love, until I met you.

"Occasionally I suggested to Mark someone else might be better for him, but he just scoffed whenever I brought it up. 'There's no one else for me but you,' he'd say. 'There never really has been.'

"I have to be fair to him and to myself. I have to find out if I can love him...the way I love you. And the longer I stay here with you, the harder it's going to be to leave." *If I can even do it now.*

Luke stood up and walked to the edge of the railing. He stared out at the water for a long time. Finally he turned toward Dana and took a deep breath. "I never thought I would be able to love anyone again, much less as much as I loved Jamie." He walked over to her, sandwiched her hands in his, and looked deeply in her eyes. "Dana, would you—"

Gently, Dana pulled her hands away and pressed her fingers against his lips. "Please, Luke," she said softly. "Don't ask me to stay. It would be too easy to say yes."

Dana put her arms around him, wanting the strength she had found through him to be with her forever.

Luke held her tightly. "Forgive me. I hadn't planned on asking you to stay until I heard my voice forming the words. In reality, though, how could I have thought I would be able to love you and just let you go?"

"I know," she whispered.

He sighed deeply and continued, "I'm glad I was able to help you, and I'm honored you chose me to do so." He held her at arm's length and looked into her eyes. "Besides, discovering I can love again—something I hadn't thought possible—well, you've touched my life as much as I've touched yours. And maybe you showed up in my life so that I could help you, and you could help *me* put my life in perspective." He kissed the tip of her nose. "I've gained new insight and understanding about myself, that's for certain." His voice choked as he added, "Though I can't honestly say it's all worth the pain of you leaving." He cleared his throat. "I guess the surprise I arranged for you today is a farewell gift."

"A surprise?" Dana smiled halfheartedly.

"Yep. Go get your camera—and don't forget your telephoto lens."

Chapter Fifteen

THE BELL JETRANGER HELICOPTER WAS WAITING WHEN THEY arrived at Luke's friend's dock a few miles away. Luke introduced Dana to Steve, the pilot.

"You've got a beautiful day for this, Dana," Steve commented.

Dana smiled. "Yes, whatever *this* is!"

"She doesn't know where we're going," Luke explained.

"A little mystery, huh?" asked Steve. "Great! Hop in, put your headsets and seat belts on, and we're off!"

The turbine engine whined as Steve increased the power and eased the helicopter off the dock. They headed first for Luke's island, hovering near the house so Dana could take photographs. Below them, Sitka ran back and forth on the deck, barking excitedly.

Banking the helicopter to the north, Steve climbed to the ridge of the mountain range that separated the bay from the next fjord. Deftly he touched down on a large, flat outcropping.

"This is breathtaking!" Dana marveled as they climbed out of the helicopter and took in the panoramic view.

"We're only at about three thousand feet here," Luke said, "but the mountains rise so steeply on either side, it feels like we're at ten thousand feet."

They hiked along the ridge. As they reached the peak, a rainbow appeared in the distance, clear and crisp in the clean air. Luke took Dana's hand and pointed out his island and the other places they'd visited. The line of volcanoes was visible in the distance.

Dana took numerous photographs of the magnificent scenery. As Luke watched her, his heart beat a bit faster. How he loved this remarkable woman! He had never met anyone so honest, genuine, determined, or courageous. Shy at first, she had surprised him with her sensuality and her passion, especially in light of her past. What she thought had been extinguished as a child had only been repressed. Like a rare and lovely flower, she had opened and flourished with the right nourishment, most of that coming from within herself.

Luke swallowed the lump in his throat, not sure he could trust his voice. "Ready?" he asked, surprised he sounded so normal.

Dana sighed. "I guess so. Though it's so beautiful from up here, I'm not sure I want to leave. And it's so quiet. All you can hear is the wind. Thank you." Dana gave him a dazzling smile, but the sadness in her eyes told him she was thinking the same thing he was: this was their last day together.

Luke helped Dana into the helicopter, his hand holding hers more tightly than necessary. They put on their seat belts and headsets, and Steve continued their flight on a northerly course.

Luke glanced over at Dana. She was clearly mesmerized by the panorama. She seemed to have managed to put aside—or at least overlook—her sadness at having to leave. At least for the time being. He was glad for that. He smiled at the childlike wonder on her face as they flew low and fast over the glaciers, looking down on immense crevasses and blue ice.

Reaching a smooth ice field, Steve landed gently and opened the door.

"It's okay to walk on this?" Dana asked, noticing a rivulet of water cascading through a crack in the ice.

"Sure. It's slippery, though. Be careful." Steve showed her how to bow her legs and walk close to the ground.

"Let's see if we can find any ice worms," Luke said.

Dana looked doubtfully from Luke to Steve.

"It's true," Steve said. "They're tiny and look like long, skinny earthworms. They live on microscopic organisms."

Dana turned slowly in a circle, awed by the massive glacier. "This is unbelievable! I've never seen anything like this."

Luke squeezed her hand.

They returned to the helicopter a few minutes later, just as the ice cracked in the distance.

Dana jumped. "That sounded like a cannon," she said.

Luke smiled. "Steve arranged that just for us."

Steve lightly punched Luke's shoulder, and Dana touched Luke's cheek. "This is truly spectacular." Dana took one last look around before climbing into the helicopter.

Steve landed the JetRanger gently on the dock and let the engine idle. Dana and Luke climbed out, ducking to avoid the rotor blades. They waved good-bye as Steve lifted off and headed back to town. As they watched the helicopter grow smaller, Dana said, "This has been the perfect end to a perfect trip. I'll never be able to thank you enough."

Luke kissed her forehead. "You already have."

Arriving at the island, Luke and Dana pulled the Zodiac onto the small beach in the cove. Coming seemingly out of nowhere, Sitka bounded down the rocks to greet them.

"Sitka!" Dana hugged him and scratched his head. "We had a wonderful time. I wish you could have joined us." She pointed to the ridge. "We were up there—on that mountain."

"Someday I'll climb that mountain with him," Luke said as he secured the boat.

"When you do, think of me."

"Dana, I'll always be thinking of you."

After a slightly awkward silence, Luke bowed deeply, determined to keep the mood light. "So, what's your pleasure, mademoiselle? Halibut, salmon, shrimp? Coffee, tea, or me?"

Dana smiled mischievously. "How about some of each? Especially you."

Laughing, Luke took Dana in his arms and kissed her deeply. Then, hand in hand, they slowly walked back to the house, stopping to eat blueberries on the way.

They kept their conversation topical and easy while they prepared dinner: an epicurean delight of halibut, salmon, crab, and shrimp. As if by unspoken consent, neither mentioned the parting that would come soon enough, though in the frequent silences, Luke—and he suspected Dana too—reflected on their time together, the joys and sorrows they had shared, the many things they had learned from each other, and how they both had changed.

After dinner, they celebrated their friendship with a bottle of vintage champagne.

"I've got something for you," Luke said, "to remind you of me."

"I won't need anything to remind me of you," Dana said, touching her heart. "You'll always be with me."

Luke felt his own heart turn over. "I'm glad. Nevertheless..." He handed her a set of wind chimes. "You can hang these on your deck."

"Oh, Luke, thank you!" Dana ran her hand through the melodious chimes. Tears filled her eyes. "The sound is as lovely as your music."

How am I going to live without her? Luke asked himself, hurting nearly as much as he had after Jamie died. But he knew he had to put Dana first. He couldn't let his feelings and desires get in the way. Because he loved her as much as he did, he wanted what was best for her. Kind of ironic, he thought. He'd helped her to release her past, and now he had to release her. But whereas she had let go of a horrible and monstrous nightmare, he was letting go of one of the most beautiful things that had ever happened to him. His voice was soft. "This is going to sound like one of those sappy cards that tell you to let the person you love go if you love them. But it's true. I love you more than I ever dreamed it would be possible to love again. But because it's what you want, I know I have to let you go. I wish you the greatest joy imaginable. And you've given me the miraculous gift of knowing I can love again."

Wordlessly, they stepped into each other's arms and clung tightly to one another.

They finally broke the embrace, and Luke, his voice cracking with emotion, said, "Why don't you soak in the hot tub one last time? I'll clean up in here."

"Let me help you," Dana offered, taking a quick swipe at her eyes with the back of her hand.

"Only take me a minute. You go enjoy the sunset. I know how much you love that hot water."

The truth of the matter was, Luke needed a few minutes to compose himself. If he were to look into Dana's beautiful face for a minute longer, he was afraid he'd lose all of his determination and beg her to stay.

Chapter Sixteen

DANA HUNG THE WIND CHIMES ON AN OVERHANGING SPRUCE bough and was immediately rewarded by soothing, tinkling music played by a gentle ocean breeze. She then set her clothes on the bench and climbed into the tub. She watched Luke through the kitchen window. How on earth would she be able to live without him? Pain gripped her heart and jumped into her throat. She couldn't bear to think about it and pushed the question out of her mind. Closing her eyes, she luxuriated in the redwood tub as the hot water massaged her body and relaxed her.

Dana's every thought was of Luke as she fell into a dreamlike state. He would always reside within her for having helped her throw off the shackles of her past and for having awoken great passion within her. Everything about him—his voice, his touch, his music, his very presence—had helped her get to where she was today: thriving and flourishing. She was gloriously alive and tuned to harmonious perfection, like the melodious wind chimes swaying above her.

The *putt-putt* of a passing fishing boat roused her from her reverie. Stepping out of the hot tub, Dana grabbed her towel and wrapped it around her. She slipped her shoes on and climbed down the stairs to the rocks by the edge of the shoreline where she liked to sit and watch the sunset. The tide was at its lowest, and in the last rays of the setting sun, she noticed an object glinting in the sand. It was a glass float, the kind that Japanese fishermen tie to their nets. She picked it up and twirled it by the short length of line still attached to the twisted webbing surrounding it.

Walking back to the house, she found Sitka resting at his favorite spot on the grassy knoll. She sat beside him, petting him, and gazed across the open ocean beyond the mouth of the bay. The volcanic range that the sun had just set behind looked like cardboard cutouts silhouetted against the brilliant orange horizon. How she would miss this beauty, this island. How she would miss this man!

She leaned against a spruce tree, unable to stop thinking about Luke. Each time they made love, their connection strengthened and deepened. Each time they melted into one, she thought she had reached the peak of sexual ecstasy and fulfillment. And each time she climbed higher.

Blinking away tears, Dana got up and returned to the deck where Luke was waiting for her.

"This is for you to remember *me*," she said as she handed him the glass ball.

Luke held up the float in the waning light. "I'll hang this in the bay window by my bed. It will be the first thing I see in the morning and the last thing I see at night."

Dana took Luke's hand in hers. "The greatest gift you've given me is loving me no matter what I told you. Thanks to you, I am truly at peace. Like this glass ball, I'm now free from what had bound me and weighed me down."

"You did it yourself, Dana."

Dana shook her head. "I couldn't have done it without you."

"All I did was help you find what was already within you."

Dana was pensive. "You know my stuffed animal, Brownie?"

Luke arched an eyebrow. "How could I forget him? I've rolled over on him more than once."

"Oh. Right. Well, I've had him since I was a little girl. I had lots of stuffed animals then. Still do, actually. Anyway, I used to sit on the floor in my bedroom and put all of my animals in a circle around me. I talked to them and confided in them. They were my friends.

"Whenever I needed to…think of something else, Brownie and my other stuffed animals took me to exciting, far-off places. They carried me to kingdoms with magnificent gardens overflowing with happy children. Sometimes we went to wide, sandy beaches where I ran on the pure white sand. Other times they took me to a grassy meadow where wild horses ran free. The same chestnut pony was always waiting for me. I climbed on her back, and together we raced through the countryside.

"During that time, I started having a dream that gave me a lot of comfort and strength. We'd be traveling then too, flying high in the sky, resting on white, fluffy clouds, traveling to the same places I visualized when I was awake. But in my nighttime dreams, we were searching for someone. Brownie was the leader of my stuffed animals, and I'd say to him, 'Brownie, you promised me. If we look long enough, you said we'd find him.' 'Be patient,' he would say to me. 'Be patient.'

"We never found him, but when I woke up from my dream, I was engulfed by a feeling of peace. I've never experienced that sense of well-being other than during this dream—until I was here with you, on your island."

Dana's eyes bored into Luke's. "And you know, when I did wake up, I knew I could make it through the day. Somehow I found the strength to continue, despite what was probably going to happen that night. The dream was my lifeboat, especially toward the end, when my uncle was threatening to kill me."

Dana took a deep breath and continued. "After my uncle

stopped hurting me, the dream became less and less frequent, eventually stopping entirely. Until I met you. After we climbed the chocolate-drop mountain, I had that dream again for the first time in almost twenty years. Actually, it was one of the reasons I decided to come over here, to the island—and to you."

Dana clutched Luke's hand. "Two nights ago I had the dream again, and Brownie said, 'Dana, you've found the person we've been searching for. That person is *you.*'"

Her voice was soft. "You've helped me to find that person, *me,* and a life filled with joy, love, and passion." She blinked away tears. "And now I need to find out how that person fits into the rest of my life."

Luke embraced her and held her for a long time.

Dana broke the silence. Pointing to the east, she exclaimed, "Look at the moon!" An enormous full moon was rising above the trees.

"Beautiful, isn't it?"

"Beautiful doesn't begin to describe it." She reached for the champagne and refilled their glasses. "Whenever I see a full moon, I'll think of you and hope you'll be thinking of me at the same time."

"You know I will be." Luke kissed her gently.

They retreated back to silence, their fingers entwined.

Finally Dana took Luke's glass out of his hand. She had been preparing herself for this for days. It would be the last night they would spend together, and she didn't want to cry or say anything trite. She would not allow herself to feel sad, but it took all of her control. She thought of everything Luke had done for her and everything they had experienced together. She concentrated on the joy and the acceptance he had brought into her life, the things he had helped her learn about herself, about life, and about love.

She focused on the fun they'd had together and the unique places he'd taken her. Her memories of this very special time of her life would always be with her. When she returned home and stared into the sunset over the ocean, she would smile, remembering, and her heart would be filled with joy.

She took Luke's hand, kissed him tenderly, and led him up the spiral staircase to his bed. She dropped her towel and helped him undress in the moonlight, memorizing every detail of his body. The feel of his skin electrified her, and she saw the same hunger burning in his eyes.

So often of late they had been consumed by an unbridled passion as they explored each other's bodies, needing to know every inch by heart, as if imprinting it on their minds. This time, they began slowly, gently. Their movements were rhythmic and natural, like the *Warm Breeze* rising and falling on the sea or the waves rolling onto the shore.

They communicated wordlessly, poignantly, with great emotion and fervor. What they shared was theirs alone, and they both knew they would never experience anything like it again. That last night they loved each other as they never had before, totally dissolving into each other as their lovemaking increased to a new crescendo of magnitude and meaning.

Morning dawned soft and quiet, as if anticipating an eventful day. A gentle mist blanketed the sky.

Dana awoke when Luke stirred and placed his arm across her breast, curving his body around hers. She had to make love with him one more time, wondering again how she was going to be able to leave him. She nudged him onto his back and moved on top of him, laying her head on his chest. They didn't talk, they didn't move; their thoughts and emotions were conveyed through the tactile sense of their bodies pressed together. All of their love and longing for each other was expressed silently; it was an incredibly intense and sensual experience that would be forever seared into Dana's memory. Physically and emotionally spent, they drifted off to sleep.

Dana awoke a short time later and slipped out of bed, listening to Luke's steady breathing. She pulled on Luke's favorite T-shirt and lightly touched the glass ball now hanging in the window by the bed, turning it in the light. Then, with Sitka by her side, she walked through the house, saying good-bye. She paused at each window, looking out at every tree, mountaintop, and slice of water within view, committing everything to memory.

Driven by a need to express what she was feeling, she walked to the piano and sat down on the antique bench. Sitka curled up nearby. Closing her eyes, Dana began playing, softly and slowly at first, then with greater intensity.

Lost in her music, she expressed her connection with this compassionate and sensitive man, reflecting the serenity she felt when she was with him. Her music conveyed her trust and surrender to him, revealing the desire and passion they shared.

Luke was dreaming. He was sailing with Dana on the *Warm Breeze.* He studied her while she trimmed the sails, wanting—even in his dream—to remember everything about her.

Gradually he became aware of a piano playing, the eloquent melody floating over the ocean from far away. It became louder and louder as he rose to consciousness, and he realized where he was and who was playing.

He got out of bed and quietly crept down the stairs until Dana was just within sight. He sat on a cedar tread and listened intently, admiring Dana's concentration and expressive music.

The beautiful story Dana told lingered long after she stopped playing. Luke hurried down the stairs and joined her on the piano bench, then gathered her in his arms.

"I love you," he said simply.

"I love you too."

Chapter Seventeen

Neither Dana nor Luke had any appetite for breakfast. They had stayed up most of the night talking, trying to think of everything they could ever want to say to each other. And yet there were a few things they could never say.

At last it was time to leave. As they motored the *Warm Breeze* across the bay, Luke put his arm around Dana, and they shared the closeness of their bodies one last time.

They decided not to say good-bye at the airport. Instead, they parted at the boat harbor. Sitka didn't understand why he couldn't follow Dana and started after her twice until Luke held him by the ruff of his neck.

When Dana reached the top of the boat ramp, the taxi was waiting for her. She looked back at Luke and Sitka. They were standing motionless on the dock, watching her. She dropped her bags on the backseat of the taxi and asked the driver to wait. Heart pounding, she ran down the ramp and threw herself into Luke's open arms. For one long moment, Dana desperately wished he would ask her to stay.

Reluctantly they released each other, their bodies slowly separating as if in slow motion, until their fingers were all that were touching. They looked longingly into each other's eyes, saying a silent and heartbreaking good-bye. Her throat aching from forcing herself not to cry, Dana walked away, the sense of Luke's touch lingering on her fingertips. This time she could not bear to look back.

As the Beechcraft 1900 took off from the airport and gained altitude for its flight to Anchorage, the *Warm Breeze* was already under way, heading back across the bay. The plane passed close enough to the sailboat that Dana could see Luke and Sitka on deck. Luke looked up and raised his hand in a partial wave. She could read his thoughts. They were the same as hers. *Take care of yourself. I'll never forget you. I love you.*

Tears welled in Dana's eyes as she considered what she was leaving behind. But she tried to focus instead on what she was returning to: a fuller life, a richer life than the one she had had before, certainly.

She tried to imagine how Mark would react to the new Dana. And she tried to imagine how different her life with him would be now. It was exciting, yet at the same time scary. Their relationship as they knew it would be forever altered. It would be like starting over or starting anew. Still, what they shared together was based on a rock-solid foundation. But would that change once Mark knew the truth about how she had been healed? Would he still be as loving and devoted once he knew she deeply loved another man?

More important, would she still feel the same way about him? If it turned out she couldn't love Mark as strongly as she loved Luke, she owed it to Mark to set him free. He deserved to be loved by someone completely and unconditionally, with no qualms or regrets.

Her heart turned over. *My dearest Luke.* She knew when the moon was full, she would sit on the deck outside her home and listen to the waves crashing on the rocks below, thinking about Luke, knowing he was thinking about her. And when the wind played a melody on the chimes he had given her, she'd connect with the remarkable man who'd helped her find life, love, and the key to her soul.

She also knew whatever her future might hold, whatever path she took, it would be a future of her making, on the path of her choice.

www.ingramcontent.com/pod-product-compliance
Lightning Source LLC
Chambersburg PA
CBHW070956120726
47910CB00004B/1266